Anywhere and Always

FALLING FOR
THE TYCOON

AURORA RUSSELL

Falling for the Tycoon
ISBN # 978-1-83943-818-9
©Copyright Aurora Russell 2019
Cover Art by Erin Dameron-Hill ©Copyright December 2019
Interior text design by Claire Siemaszkiewicz
Totally Bound Publishing

FALLING FOR THE TYCOON

Dedication

To my own personal lighthouse keeper, I love and appreciate you. To my boys, you are the joy that makes every day an adventure. To my dad, my mom, my stepmom, my brother and my brother's awesome wife, you have always believed in and encouraged me, and you'll never know how much that means to me. You are never far from my thoughts or my heart. To my wonderful, supportive friends, without whom life would be so much less fun. To my husband's amazing family, which I am incredibly lucky to count myself a part of. And to my sister-in-law's fabulous family members, who know how to have one heck of a good time on a train and anywhere else!

Chapter One

The sky was a perfect unending blue, clear and brilliant, its beauty rivaled only by the magnificent expanse of bright aqua ocean and baby-powder-fine sand. It had always been Annelise's dream to see the Caribbean, and she knew she should have been happy. Ecstatic. Wasn't she still here, even if she was alone? But, instead, she just felt empty. Detached.

She'd cried her tears. So many tears. For weeks. Wondering what had gone wrong to make Kyle decide to walk out on their life together, ending their wedding and honeymoon plans abruptly. Wondering what would come next. Looking at the space where his toothbrush used to sit next to the bathroom sink, looking at the empty space in the fridge where the special espresso he loved had always been kept, she'd felt a gnawing, painful ache in her chest, raw like a sucking wound. She'd sobbed into her pillow, worried she'd alarm the neighbors in the condo above. Her hot tears signaled the end of not just a seven-year-long relationship, but also of her dreams for the future. She'd cried so much she'd gone numb.

She'd managed the chores of daily living—making food, getting dressed, going to work and to the store—but she'd felt like an imposter, like some zombie trapped inside the body of the vivacious, happy, hopeful woman she'd always been. She'd looked in the mirror and it had scared her. But still, nothing moved her anymore—not sadness, not anger, not understanding or judgment. Nothing. When the reminder from the travel agency had come through as an alert on her smartphone, the hot swell of anger had been as surprising as it had been fleeting. That spark was what had led her to do the crazy thing she'd done. Just to feel something, anything, she'd decided to take their honeymoon. Alone.

Logically, the decision had been clear. She should go—two weeks in a remote section of the Yucatan Peninsula, staying at an exclusive hotel right on the beach. It was a two-hour-long ride in a Jeep on bumpy roads through the jungle to get to the collection of luxury cabanas, perched right at the edge of a wild natural preserve. Quite a journey, but it was supposed to be worth it. This was her dream trip, and it was almost entirely paid for already...and non-refundable. When they'd booked it, she hadn't even had a nanosecond of concern about that portion of the terms and conditions. The idea that Kyle would have chosen not to go would have been laughable to her on that long-ago morning. After seven years of blissful love, she'd thought she'd known him inside and out. She had never been more wrong.

The decision to come had been more complex. Could she handle the possible emotional roller-coaster of going on what was supposed to be the romantic trip of a lifetime by herself? Was she crazy to risk putting herself through a possible ordeal of 'what-ifs' and 'might-have-beens'? But when she'd looked down at that small phone screen, slightly smudged from her fingers, and had again seen the hollow, eerie eyes in her dark reflection, she'd known. She was going to go. Her best friend, Marina, was the only one who seemed to understand and support her decision. Everyone else just looked at her like she'd lost her mind.

She hadn't been able to muster much enthusiasm for the packing, but still, even just knowing that she was packing to go had made her feel a little less frozen. Instead of staring at the same walls where she'd hung pictures with Kyle, or sitting on the same couch they'd spent several happy hours picking out at the furniture store, she would escape — or so she'd thought. But of course, she couldn't ever escape. Not really. She couldn't run away from herself.

So here she stood, looking at the prettiest view she'd ever seen, hands-down. The warm breeze ruffled her hair and the air held the delicate scent of tropical flowers mixed with the tangy salt of the ocean. Even the sound of the waves lapping onto the soft sand was exquisite. Soothing. And she could appreciate it all, but only in the abstract. Here in paradise, she was still frozen. Annelise sighed and turned, determined to keep walking until she began to thaw, even if it was just a little. Maybe seeing the jungle would help. She'd read there were even toucans. She sighed again, more heavily this time, trying to feel a glimmer of her usual optimism. Marina's voice replayed in her head, encouraging her. And with Marina's own past sadness, her advice meant even more.

'Go on, girl,' her friend had said. *'Don't let that man take one more day of your life. You have too much in you left to*

give. Go wild! Do anything and everything because you never know what's around the corner.'

With those words in mind, Annelise doggedly continued, sinking her heels into the softer sand farther away from the waterline. It truly was incredible to be alone in such an unbelievably beautiful spot, and she hadn't seen another soul all day. She turned her face to the water again as she walked, watching as the sky lit up into a symphony of purples, pinks and oranges as the sun began to dip toward the horizon. Without warning, she fell over something large on the ground, landing squarely on a warm, hard object, which gave a startled grunt.

She scrambled up as quickly as possible, but not before she pressed up against the length of a tall, muscular man. He was warm and smelled of the ocean and the wind—and also a bit spicy, like some of the more exotic seasonings used in the local dishes. As she brushed herself off and stood as swiftly as she could, she just had time to realize that he smelled…incredibly good. *For someone I apparently fell on like a ton of bricks. Smooth. Real smooth, Annelise.*

"I'm so sorry!" she apologized, feeling a hot blush rise from her hairline to her ears and even onto her chest. She knew her cheeks must be flaming.

The stranger, dressed only in faded board shorts that might have been red once but were now a washed-out salmon, was covered in sand. It dusted his tan, muscular chest and sprinkled his dark-brown hair. He might have looked silly if he hadn't been… Well, the only words that sprang to her mind were 'unbelievably gorgeous'. No, that wasn't true. She also thought 'scrumptious' and 'hot as hell'. Mentally recalling herself, she realized he hadn't responded to her apology.

"Do you speak English? *Español*?" Annelise hoped he spoke at least a tiny bit of English, because her Spanish was abysmal. "Oh my gosh, did I hurt you?" she continued, worried.

The man sat up with a little shake, and his mouth quirked into a wry smile, making his dark eyes crinkle at the corners. "No apology needed. I must have fallen asleep. I'm fine. No harm done. Although"—he gestured at the empty beach—"it was an unlucky coincidence that you should choose this one spot to walk onto." His accent sounded French, and his tone was compelling as he spoke, inviting her to share his amusement, not only at their situation but also possibly at life in general.

Annelise felt an unfamiliar smile tug at the corners of her lips. "I'm so glad you're not hurt. And 'unlucky' should be my middle name," she answered, the words out before she could recall them. It was totally unlike her to talk about her personal life with a complete stranger. Alone. On a deserted beach. *Totally* alone. She took an unconscious step backward.

The stranger didn't look as though he'd been lying in wait to trip unsuspecting tourists, though. He looked as if he belonged—and as if he was mildly interested in what she was saying. If he'd looked too interested, she might have shut down, but instead, she found herself answering the questioning quirk of his dark eyebrow.

"I've...had a bit of a setback recently in my personal life," she said. It was the understatement of the century.

"Sounds like it was a bad one. Do you want to talk about it?" he offered, as if it were the most natural thing in the world, just two strangers watching a Caribbean sunset and talking about their personal lives. It suddenly occurred to her that he was the first person besides the unobtrusive security guards that she'd seen on the private beach this entire trip. She'd actually begun to think she must be the only guest at the cabanas. Her thoughts turned suddenly suspicious.

"What are you doing on this beach? It's supposed to be private and definitely a no-trespassing sort of place." Her mind turned to the prominent guns she'd seen the security guards carrying, and she wasn't sure if she was trying to intimidate or warn the stranger.

The white of his smile on his tan face was stunning in the sunset. "Thank you for the warning, *cherie*, but I am a guest here…in the owner's cabana." He gestured with one long, muscular arm and Annelise noticed a path she hadn't seen before, leading to what looked like a giant house. It was much larger than her own spacious cabin.

"Oh, right. The owner's French, isn't he?" Annelise answered, trying to recall the details she knew of the resort. She'd learned about it from her colleague, and the owner was a big-time client of the financial services firm where she worked.

"French-Canadian," the stranger corrected, raising his eyebrow again, "but I'll let it slide just this once."

"Sorry…I know there's a big difference," she hastened to apologize. Great, she'd now offended a close friend of a client who could get her fired.

The stranger shook his head. "I was teasing. I'm not so easily offended," he said, bending up his knees and wrapping his arms loosely around them before motioning toward the soft-looking hollow next to him. "Care to join me? You can't beat the view."

Again, his offer was casual. Careless, almost. But somehow that put Annelise at ease when she hadn't been remotely at ease, anywhere, in months. He had a beautiful voice, dark and rumbling, deep and masculine. It was a good match for his tall, broad frame.

"You've already been on top of me. Is it so bad to be next to me?" He waggled his eyebrows in an exaggerated way, and the bark of laughter that escaped her shocked her so much that she put a hand to her mouth. She sat down more out of shock than anything else.

"I...can't believe you made me laugh. I haven't...felt like laughing in months." She spoke her thoughts aloud, almost forgetting she wasn't alone. Strange, but she felt such an instant camaraderie with the stranger that she already thought of him as a sort of friend.

"The owner told me that there was supposed to be a couple on their wedding trip these weeks. But I have seen you alone?" He made the statement a question.

Annelise felt some of the familiar grief at the word 'wedding', but somehow, it felt muted this time. She nodded slowly. "Yes, my fiancé Kyle left me three months before our wedding. We'd been together for seven years, so it was a surprise. I...thought we were in love. I loved him, very much. But he... His note said he didn't want the same things anymore."

"*Quel conard...putain de merde.*"

Annelise was surprised at the vehemence in his voice. It was real anger. It didn't make her nervous, though. He sounded like she often felt toward Kyle.

"I, ah...don't remember my high-school French all that well, but I'm guessing what you just said wasn't very nice."

The stranger's easy grin split his face again, and it made him so handsome, even in the growing shadows of dusk, that it almost took her breath away. Still, she could see a real anger and pain behind the geniality.

"I hope they don't teach these words in high-school French." He looked back out at the water, and the light blazed pink and red across his cheeks. "I said he was a fool. Well, something like that."

Annelise raised her eyebrows. "I appreciate it, but I could be awful, you know."

The man shrugged. A beautifully Gallic shrug that could mean anything. "You could be, but I don't think you are. The catch in your voice, the sadness in your eyes... You loved this fiancé very much. You were committed. He hurt you."

His words hung in the sunset, heavy with meaning. He understood. Somehow, Annelise felt how much he really understood.

"What was her name?" she guessed.

"*His* name," he corrected.

Annelise was genuinely surprised, though of course she shouldn't have been. A man that handsome, flirting so openly with her. "Ah...naturally. *His* name. I understand," she echoed.

The stranger's chuckle came again, rich and deep with amusement. "So sorry, *petite*. *Non*, you don't understand. The fault is mine, not yours. I have never had the good fortune to find love with anyone. Claude is the name of the man who broke my sister's heart. We trusted him, you see, like a brother. But he was only interested in..." He broke off as if searching for the right words.

"Sex? Fun? A good time?" Annelise suggested, the words out before she realized how much she was revealing.

The man raised one eyebrow at her words. "Good guesses. Most interesting, but no. He wanted money." He paused, looking out again at the water, his face growing harder to see in the deepening obscurity. "*Non*, that's not true. He had money already, but he wanted much more of it — and power. He saw that the only way to take it from us was through our jewel. Our *trésor*. Clothilde, our only sister. She was still a girl when they met, and she loved him. We all did. His betrayal drove a knife into the heart of our family, and we bleed still."

The words should have sounded melodramatic. Instead, the way the man spoke with his slight accent, getting thicker as his emotions rose, sounded truthful, and sad. Sympathy welled within her, yet another surprising feeling for someone who'd feared she was permanently frozen.

"I'm so sorry." She stopped as her words seemed inadequate. "That's not enough... I truly comprehend what you've gone through, and I feel for you." Her hand went to her chest, over her heart, without conscious thought.

The stranger touched her free hand. Such a light touch, then it was gone, but it set off a chain reaction of nerves blinking to life after long lying dormant. Annelise had thought — and feared — that she would never feel such a tingling awareness of a man again.

"Thank you," he said, and his words were low with sincerity.

"How is your sister...Clothilde?" Annelise asked, sure she was getting the pronunciation wrong but still wanting to try. When he said it, it sounded like *Cloh-teeld*.

"It has been six months, and we still worry that she hasn't decided whether to come back or give up. She just...pretends to live. She walks around and does everything she is supposed to, but she's like an automaton. A phantom. Behind her eyes, where there was always joy and a sparkle, now we see only pain — or worse, nothing."

Annelise was stunned at how close his words hit to her own feelings, the ambivalence she hadn't been able to shake off.

"We have taken turns, my brothers and I, spending time with her and trying to coax her smiles, but it is...difficult." He sighed, a heavy, frustrated sound, then turned back to her, almost as if he'd just recalled himself. "But I wanted to hear about you, to perhaps lighten your pain in the way that only an outside listener can do, not put my burdens onto you. I'm Rémy, by the way. May I know your name, *ma belle*?"

Annelise was surprised to feel herself blush again, as if she'd never been complimented before...by a tall, dark, seductive stranger on a beach straight out of her wildest dreams. Okay, maybe she never *had* been complimented like that before. She smiled at the silliness of her own thoughts.

"Annelise," she answered, holding out her hand automatically, which seemed ridiculous, given the intimacy of the dark beach, just starting to lighten again with moonrise. Rémy didn't seem to notice her sudden awkwardness, though, as he took her hand and held it to his lips. They were hot and soft when he briefly touched the back of her hand to them as if it were the most natural thing in the world to kiss a total stranger.

"What a beautiful name. *Enchanté*, Annelise," he murmured, and suddenly she couldn't contain the peal of laughter that escaped her.

He looked up at her in surprise, the dark-chocolate brown of his eyes almost fathomless in the darkness, questioning.

"I thought French...or French-Canadian men only said that in movies. I mean, you really kiss hands and say that? That's an actual *thing*?" She was shocked at her own teasing, at how uninhibited she felt, bold in the dim evening.

An answering glint of amusement crept into Rémy's eyes, even though he kept his face serious. "That is most definitely a... What did you call it? A thing? I'm just glad I didn't kiss you on the cheek twice or three times like I would if we'd met in Paris or Provence. You would have fallen over with mirth." He paused speculatively. "Actually, I would have enjoyed that very much."

Annelise couldn't help but laugh again. Now that she was amused, it seemed she couldn't stop. "What, kissing my cheeks or watching me fall over?"

Rémy's voice was dark velvet. "Both, *chérie*. But mostly hearing your laughter and seeing you smile."

He sounded sincere, and Annelise was touched.

"I saw you yesterday, and earlier today, from across the beach. You looked so very sad. Lost."

Annelise hugged her knees and felt the warm, soft breeze tugging at her hair. For almost the first time since she'd been in Mexico, she could enjoy it. "I *was* sad, and lost, but I think I'm finding my way back. Thank you, Rémy." She was curiously reluctant to get up and end the strange, yet somehow significant, interlude. Or maybe she just didn't want to leave the kindest, funniest man she'd ever met — who also happened to be hot as hell. *And am I imagining the desire I've seen a couple of times in his expression?* If so, she didn't care. It felt amazing.

Rémy seemed to share her reluctance. "I'll walk you to your cabana. It's dark, but I know the beach very well."

She looked at him skeptically from under her eyelashes. "There's enough moonlight, and it's really not that far."

He shrugged again. "Humor me, *petite*. Otherwise, I might worry." His tone was light, but she thought she heard real concern, too.

The idea of such a big, confident man worried about a stranger he'd happened across — or, rather, who'd happened across him by literally tripping over him — was almost laughable. On the other hand, he was honestly very worried about his sister and he'd been sensitive and caring. She felt better with him than she had for months.

"All right," she agreed, going with her gut instead of her head. It felt right.

He rose in one fluid motion that she thought she might have to be jealous of, then saved her the ignominy of scrambling to her feet by reaching out a hand to help her. When they touched again, she felt another arc of electric awareness shoot throughout her body, bringing her nerve endings painfully back to life. *Good Lord, the man is attractive. Devastatingly. Dangerously.* Her inner voice whispered, *Why can't I enjoy him as long as I protect myself?*

That inner voice, which also sounded uncannily like her best friend, seemed to rule as they walked across the powdery sand, cooled by the sunset, toward her cabana. Where before she'd mostly felt her own misery, now she appreciated the texture of the sand between her toes, the lush smell of the ocean mingled with the tropical jungle nearby and she was lulled and calmed by the gentle lapping of the waves onto the shore. When Rémy took her hand, it felt natural, an extension of the intimacy they'd already created, talking as candidly as they had in the evening shadows. They seemed to slow their steps, making the walk last longer than it normally would.

Her heart sank when they stopped in front of her little cabin, and she felt oddly bereft that the small interlude was coming to an end. "Here we are," she whispered, her voice unusually husky.

"Here we are," Rémy agreed. He let go of her fingers and ran his hand slowly up her arm, leaving goosebumps in the wake of his warm fingers. "I like you, lovely Annelise. I'm so glad we met."

If he'd said something flirtatious, she would have dismissed his words entirely, but he sounded like he was speaking his thoughts out loud. Something warm expanded within her chest, and she realized with shock that it was happiness, maybe even joy. She felt alive and vibrant, optimistic and excited. She felt like herself.

"Would you like to come in?" Like they were spoken by somebody else, the words were out of her mouth before she'd even thought them consciously, but as they hung there, she realized she didn't want to take them back. She knew Rémy understood what they meant. What she offered. And, suddenly, there wasn't anything in the world she wanted more than to hold this man in her arms, if only for one night. She felt daring and powerful.

Even in the silvery moonlight, she could see she'd surprised him. But then his eyes darkened and his expression changed. "Absolutely," he said, his tone gravelly, and he crushed her to him, covering her lips with his.

Chapter Two

Rémy couldn't decide what he liked most about Annelise. She seemed funny and kind, and with her long, dark hair, intelligent blue eyes and lush curves lovingly hugged by her swimsuit underneath her flowing dress, she was certainly attractive — everything he liked best in a woman, in fact, but in an understated way. He'd seen many beautiful women before, glamorous and charming, eager to catch his attention at the countless events he attended, but from the moment he'd seen Annelise from across the beach, he'd been more than attracted. He'd been absolutely drawn to her. He'd hoped for a way to meet her without intruding on what had obviously been some sort of grief, so when she'd woken him earlier — all soft, sweet-smelling woman pressed to him for an instant — he'd thought he'd been dreaming. Now, he had the same surreal sensation again at her unexpected boldness.

When she'd asked if he wanted to come in, he'd thought at first he'd imagined the words. But no, their vibrations still practically hung in the air, and the look on her face, equal parts stunned and aware, confirmed it. She had definitely asked him in — and not just to chat.

His body hardened so fast it was almost painful, and suddenly he couldn't stand the small distance between them. Her mouth beneath his was soft and she tasted sweet and a little salty. *Absolutely delicious.* Even better, she moaned and leaned into him so that he could feel every warm, luscious inch of her front pressed against him from his chest down to his thighs. She fit there, as if she were made for him, the perfect complement to his lean hardness. She kissed just the way he thought she might do everything — warm, generous and passionate.

Some small shred of sanity made him pull back, though. She gave a little sigh of disappointment when he broke their kiss, and he couldn't quite bear to fully separate them. He couldn't resist running his fingers through the silken waterfall of her hair, either, and she turned her cheek into his palm.

"You're so beautiful, Annelise, and sexy. But, are you certain this is what you want?" Despite his rising desire, the last thing he wanted was to take advantage of her sadness in any way or to end up hurting her more. She didn't deserve that.

Her eyes flashed quickly with hurt before she looked down, and he knew he'd blundered. He cupped her chin gently with his rough hand, wanting her to see him and understand.

"*Non, non, chérie.* You imagine something I did not intend. I want you." He knew those last words were gruff, but damn it, he felt a little wild. Something about her drove him a little crazy. He, who was normally so controlled, so able to withstand the charms of almost any woman, was almost panting with need for this quiet near-stranger. But he didn't only feel desire for her.

"I want you. Don't think for one second that I don't," he continued, more composed this time. "But I really do like you, too, and I would never want to hurt you. Are you certain you're ready? I can only promise you a brief time, and I would not wish to do anything to slow your heart from mending."

He must have convinced her that he spoke the truth because her lovely eyes held warmth again and she relaxed into his arms. "Thanks for explaining — and for worrying. Of course I haven't thought about it in the context of 'us'. I mean, I surprised myself with my own words a minute ago. But I think I've been thinking about something like this for a couple of months. Like, what would I do if maybe I'm not as deadened inside as I feared? And what I thought was, if I'm fortunate enough to feel such desire again, I'm seizing it with both hands. God, I want so much to feel like a woman again. Sexy, soft, desirable... Giving and taking pleasure from the man I choose. I'm not expecting forever or a happily-ever-after. I'm not even expecting tomorrow. More than anything, I know now how everything — all the most careful plans — can shift in the blink of an eye. I want this...*you*...for as long as we have...if you're still interested."

Her words made sense, and she reaffirmed everything he'd suspected about her. When she wasn't grieving the loss of her dreams with her idiot of an ex, she was exquisitely smart and passionate. *Mon Dieu*, she was something to behold. She truly wanted this and he certainly wasn't going to stop her.

"Interested?" He kissed her, a short kiss full of promise and dark sensuality, so that her face was a little dazed when he raised his head again. "*Chérie*, if I got any more interested, we'd both go up in flames." He stroked her back through the thin fabric of her dress, and felt her answering shiver with deep satisfaction. His little Annelise was just as responsive as he'd hoped.

"One more thing... I don't have protection, though I can assure you I'm clean," he said, wanting to be protective of her, even if it meant walking away from something he now wanted with every molecule of his body.

Her blush grew deeper. "I'm, um...clean too, and still on the pill, so we don't have to worry about that. And...I trust you."

Rémy trusted her, too, as if he'd known her for much longer. As if instead of meeting her tonight, he'd found an old friend. Well, an old friend who was also unbelievably sexy and made him hard as a rock.

"*Bébé*, I am going to make this *so* good for you," he growled, and scooped her up into his arms to take her inside.

Rémy was *carrying* her. Annelise didn't think she could remember being carried by anyone, certainly not Kyle. It should have felt presumptuous, and it was definitely a caveman move, but oh, Lord, it just felt hot, like he wanted her so badly he couldn't stand it. Her core went liquid as she wrapped her arms around his neck. His chest and arms felt hard and corded with muscles, and even though she wasn't a lightweight, his breathing didn't even change as he carried her. She was so focused on how damn strong he was that it took her a second to realize he wasn't taking her to the enormous, mosquito-net-enshrouded bed. Instead — and she could only see by the light of the small lamp she'd left on — it looked like he was taking her to the...kitchen?

"I think you're going the wrong way," she said softly. The look he flashed down at her was pure heat.

"No mistake, *chérie*. The kitchen is always my favorite place to eat."

Her body flushed all over as his meaning sank in. She had only a second to think before she felt the cool marble of the high-countered breakfast bar underneath the thin fabric of her cover-up. Then his mouth was on hers again, caressing her and making her lose all rational thought. At the same time, he raised one hand again to her hair, massaging her scalp, and skimmed another over her breast, feathering her nipple. She moaned against his mouth at the combination of sensations, and her nipples hardened to brazen little peaks, begging for attention where they pressed against his bare chest.

Rémy, the gentleman that he was, stepped close to stand between her legs, which she promptly wrapped around him. She tunneled her fingers into his thick, dark hair, marveling at how unexpectedly soft it was. When she ran her nails lightly down his bare back, it was his turn to moan. Their ragged breathing was loud in the quiet of the cabana, the only other sound the distant waves and the gentle sea breeze through the palm trees.

Rémy caught her gaze with his, intent and questioning, as he raised his mouth from hers and reached for the knots of her bathing suit top. Somehow, he'd already slipped the bodice of her gauzy cover-up dress off and it had fallen to her waist, leaving only her bikini top separating their bare skin.

"Please," she whispered, answering his unspoken question, and he needed no further encouragement. He untied the fastening with deft fingers and nearly growled with satisfaction as her large breasts spilled free. They bobbled for a mere instant before he covered them with his rough hands. Annelise had thought her nipples couldn't get harder or more sensitive, but at the feeling of his lightly callused fingers on the soft skin of her breasts, they tightened to diamonds, and she panted with each brush of his skin against them.

"Gorgeous," he breathed, his voice a mere rasp of sound, before he bent his dark head to pull one nipple into the molten heat of his mouth. Annelise let her head fall back in ecstasy while she cradled his head to her chest. She didn't think anything had ever felt so good.

"Oh my God." Her words were a mere whisper of sound, but he must have heard them.

"You like that?" he rumbled, the vibration of his voice against her breast nearly sending her over the edge.

"Yes," she gasped, pulling on his hair, urging him on.

His dark chuckle was full of promise. "Not too fast, *bébé*. I want you to enjoy every second."

He took his time, laving first one stiff peak then the other, each pull of his mouth, combined with the strokes of his hands, driving her higher until she thought she might snap from the glorious tension. Just when she thought she couldn't stand any more, Rémy laid her down, right on the cool stone counter.

He put a soft dishtowel under her head, the gesture so incongruously tender that she felt a warm glow, then pulled the rest of her cover-up and bathing suit off together in one deft motion, baring her waist, hips and wet core to him. The height of the counter was tall, so that when he coaxed open her thighs, he could look directly at her, already wet and swollen for him.

Annelise had never been entirely comfortable receiving oral sex. It made her feel brazen and shameless in a way she'd never been with a partner before, particularly after Kyle had mentioned that he just wasn't into the look, smell or taste of her. But the expression on Rémy's face was intense and filled with desire, underlaid with a kind of worship.

"You are…sexy everywhere," he said, his voice low and intent.

Annelise spread her thighs so wide that the muscles stretched. She was feeling unbelievably desirable, offering herself to him. His gaze flashed to hers, and she went breathless at what she saw. His face was a mask of need, but every line of his body held tenderness, too. He was going to be wild, she could tell, but every bit of this would be for both of them.

Rémy inhaled as though he savored her scent, which she found even sexier. Then, without preamble, he buried his face between her thighs, and she couldn't think of anything else any longer. She was pure sensation. His tongue and fingers seemed to be everywhere at once, stroking up and down her slit and skimming over her most sensitive bundle of nerves lightly, tantalizingly. He drank from her as someone parched, who might never get enough.

She thrashed her head back and forth as he took her higher and higher. Her little cries of pleasure echoed off the walls of the kitchen as she hurtled toward ecstasy, too consumed with desire to be amazed at how quickly he'd aroused her. When he made a deep sound of satisfaction right against her clit, his low voice vibrating, and curled one capable finger into her wet sheath, it was too much. She went white-hot all over, tensing then exploding into a million sparkling pieces of pleasure.

While she was still in a haze of bliss, Rémy flipped her over. Dimly, she marveled at how strong he must be for the movement to be so effortless. He bent her over the counter, feathering kisses along her spine as his hands skimmed her sides and legs, leaving goosebumps in their wake. He kissed the side of her neck and she shivered.

"I thought to take a long time, to draw this out for hours," he said in a guttural voice so close to her ear that her hair tickled her neck. "I don't think I can wait, *chérie*, so I hope you're ready now."

She felt the hard length of his cock pressing against the soft mounds of her bottom. He felt enormous and amazing. A perfect fit.

"Oh yes," she breathed. If he had asked her to dance naked outside, she would have done it. She felt that good. "Now, Rémy. *Please.*"

That was all the encouragement he needed as he tore off his shorts then drove into her in one long stroke. She was so wet that he slid in easily, fully, filling her deeply and completely. She screamed and braced herself on the counter with her forearms, the movement causing her nipples to brush against the cold, smooth polished marble, which ratcheted up her desire again to a fever pitch, as though she hadn't come a short while earlier.

"Yes, oh, yes," she said, wiggling her hips a little to urge him to move.

Rémy held still for a moment longer, every muscle taut, clearly struggling for control. Then he stroked in and out, slowly at first, so that every inch of his hard cock dragged against all of the sensitive nerve endings of her passage. Annelise thought she might just go up in flames or melt into a puddle at his feet. Nothing had ever felt so perfect.

"So. Good." She panted the words in time with his rhythm.

Rémy moved his hands to her hips then reached around to pinch her nipples and rub them, sending jolts of pleasure directly to her pussy. He bent his head to her neck again to kiss her tenderly, even as his hips moved faster and faster until his cock drove into her at a wild pace. She loved it. She wanted more. *Needed* more.

He seemed to understand her wordless cries, and he responded, moving even faster. The combination of his skin, sliding against her own sweat-dampened skin, contrasted with the cool, smooth marble of the countertop, heightened her senses, and she threw her head back. With every stroke, she felt stretched deliciously, totally filled, as if their pleasure combined and magnified, hot and wild, sparkling and burning out of control until she abandoned herself to it completely.

Just when she thought she might explode, he drove into her and reached down to caress her clit, sending her flying again into complete ecstasy. Her orgasm broke over her like a wave, crashing and rippling, like nothing she'd ever felt before, until tears prickled her eyes.

Rémy was relentless behind her, inside her, drawing out her pleasure with his pounding rhythm, every stroke making her gasp and moan, shivering all over. Finally, he drove into her, hard, three more times, then grunted with pure satisfaction, his muscles growing taut behind her, shooting jet after jet of his hot, creamy seed deep into her. Her inner walls rippled around him as he somehow maneuvered her back onto the counter and she half-collapsed into his arms.

She didn't know how long she lay there. It could have been a minute or an hour. But Rémy continued gently stroking her pussy, drawing out the little quakes that still made her tremble with pleasure. He feathered caresses over her thighs with his other hand as she came back to herself.

"Oh my God," she groaned, flushing with a prickly heat all over at how totally abandoned she'd been.

"Close, *ma belle*. Rémy, but you can call me 'God' if you want to," he teasingly corrected.

Annelise couldn't contain the full-on snort of amusement that escaped her, and she gasped as her movement made her clit brush, ever so slightly, against his finger, causing another mini-explosion. Mortified, she tried to close her thighs, but Rémy's hands held her, gently but firmly.

"I like the way you snort, *chérie*, and the way you scream. It means you are real…and truly enjoying yourself."

Annelise lifted her head to look at him. She didn't think she'd ever seen anything sexier. His thick, dark hair was tousled and wind-blown, his eyes were earnest and warm with desire and his magical lips were still slightly swollen

"How could I *not* enjoy myself? You must know you're incredible. I just… I'm not normally like this."

Rémy cocked one dark eyebrow. "Like what? A sexy goddess of the sea, created just to seduce men?"

She felt like laughing again at the absurdity of his words. "Well, yeah. That's… No one has ever thought anything like that about me."

"Maybe they didn't know you very well." He looked at her searchingly, suddenly serious. "Maybe your…Kyle, was it? Maybe he didn't know you very well — or he never could have left."

His words hung in the room, but before Annelise had decided how to respond, he changed the subject.

"Speaking of sea goddesses, you would look incredible wearing only moonlight and water, no? Would you like to try it?" His dark eyes were at once full of laughter and lingering desire.

Annelise had secretly always wanted to go skinny-dipping, but she'd never been, not even as a child growing up in the suburbs. She was tempted, but something still held her back. "What about the other guests? Or guards? Wouldn't they see us?"

The slow grin that spread across Rémy's face was full of satisfaction. He knew he'd won her over. *And, Lord, why shouldn't I let him?* He stood there, not wearing a stitch, and looked as comfortable as if he never wore clothes. *He sure doesn't need to*, she thought, *with all those chiseled muscles and tan skin*. And he was all but offering to be hers for the rest of the night, too. *Why the hell not? What do I have to lose?* On the flipside, she had everything to gain.

"I know for a fact there's no one else here as a guest tonight, and I know the guards. I'll ask them not to disturb us." His voice was husky, and Lord if her body didn't give a little quiver of arousal at the promise in his tone. She flushed warm again at her own thoughts.

Rémy pulled on his shorts so they hung low on his hips, not bothering to button them, and his dark chuckle as he turned let her know he hadn't missed her reaction. "I'll go find one now, *petite*, and they all have intercoms." He turned to leave, then quickly ran back to her, kissing her full on the mouth. "Don't think too much. Just feel." He tapped her lightly on the forehead, then he was gone, taking off at a run into the glittering moonlight.

Chapter Three

Alone in the cabana, Annelise was equal parts shocked and pleased with herself. Or mostly just pleased? As she pulled on another flimsy gauze cover-up that highlighted her curves — because she was *naked* and had shown every bit of herself to a near-stranger who looked like he had stepped right out of a magazine or movie — she was incredulous at her own daring. And yet, she liked it. She liked how she felt, and for the first time in months — or maybe even years — she felt like she wasn't compromising. She was an independent woman who did whatever she wanted, especially if what she wanted was named Rémy! She laughed at her own thoughts.

This was part of letting go, she reasoned. For years, ever since she and Kyle had gotten serious, she'd thought, planned and committed to never have an experience like this. She had given up the chance to meet anyone else, and she'd given it up gladly. But this was an unexpected upside of being newly-single. She didn't know how good she'd be at the whole 'no future' thing and keeping an emotional distance, but she was damn willing to try if it meant the unbridled passion and pleasure Rémy had shown her. She would simply guard her heart and keep everything light. They obviously lived in different cities, different countries, and they were both on vacation, so anything more than this night, or a couple of nights, was simply not happening. Subject closed. *Mostly.*

Rémy had guessed Annelise would be passionate, but he'd had no idea of how deeply passionate she would be as a lover. She'd inflamed him like none of the models and glamorous society beauties he'd been with before ever had, with her innocent and honest responses. She was earthy and sensual, and he could tell that she'd really enjoyed herself. He realized that she might be the first woman he'd been with who had allowed herself to be so abandoned. What had started as a desire to meet her and maybe take away some of her sorrow — something he was extra attuned to lately with Clothilde's recent heartbreak — had turned into something much different and more personal. He liked her, was wildly attracted to her and wanted to spend as much time as possible with her. Period.

His family hadn't become the most successful business owners in their high-tech field without learning how to be relentless in their pursuit of what they wanted, and whether he understood his reasons or not, he wanted Annelise. Badly. His body hardened even thinking of her, and he couldn't wait to see her naked in the warm, clear ocean, drenched with moonlight and water. He hurried his steps at the thought.

He'd already grabbed one of the guards, Manuel, and advised him not to disturb them under any circumstances. Manuel's eyes had widened and he'd understood. He knew who Rémy was and he'd listen to his request, which was really an order, since he wanted to keep his well-paying job. Rémy's brother, Pierre, the owner of all the cabanas, might chide him when he heard about it, but screw it. Rémy didn't often feel this way — maybe had *never* felt this way — and he wasn't going to let Annelise be scared off because he hadn't been clear with the guards. He realized that he truly cared about her feelings, and he didn't want her embarrassed. He, the consummate playboy, didn't want his shy goddess blushing. He was the only one he wanted making her blush.

When he got back to the cabana, he was relieved to see that she still appeared happy to see him. She'd put something on, which he thought was too bad, but then his breath caught as he really looked at what she wore. It looked demure enough at first glance, another gauzy cover-up, but it clung to her lovingly, like a second skin, and draped everywhere to accentuate her generous hips and breasts. His mouth watered. Even better, it was so thin that he could tell she hadn't put on any underwear. He could just make out the darkness of her rose-tipped nipples and the thatch of golden-brown curls at the apex of her thighs. His goddess hadn't lost her nerve after all.

"Stunning, *chérie*. The moonlight is lovely, but you are even lovelier." He enjoyed how her eyes sparkled and her lips twitched at his outrageous compliment. Her gaze went to the fastening of his shorts and he loved that he could read her so clearly. He went to her and wrapped his arms around her, smelling the faint vanilla scent of her hair and the salt on her skin.

"Ready?" he asked.

She nodded, seeming suddenly shy again. Her blue eyes, though, were warm and willing. Sparkling. Her lips were still swollen from his kisses, and she looked irresistible.

When she gave a small nod, he surprised her by swinging her up into his arms again, enjoying the soft feel of her luscious body in his arms. He felt like a conqueror, and her laughing protests were half-hearted. She liked it, too. He walked them right down to the edge of the water, and as he stepped in, she squealed in surprise as he went right in up to his waist without taking their clothes off.

When he bent his knees, dunking her from the neck down, she clutched at his neck.

"What was that for?" she asked.

He looked down, noting that her cover-up had gone nearly translucent with the water. "I had to see your breasts again, and I knew they would look stunning when this thing got wet." She laughed, throwing her head back at his matter-of-fact tone. "And I was right. They do," he finished, waggling his eyebrows.

"Has anyone ever told you you're bossy? Or incorrigible?" she teased.

He shrugged. "Everyone who works for me is too scared to tell me how bossy I am. Incorrigible...maybe? But I'm too busy being bossy to pay attention." With that, he let them fall backward into the saltwater, the top layer still warmed from the day. She squealed in surprise before it was muffled as he went underwater.

When he surfaced, she was spluttering and stood, wringing out her long hair. "A little warning might have been nice," she said accusingly, but her eyes were still twinkling. As she walked back a short way then turned to look at him, he didn't know if he had ever seen anyone so beautiful...or seductive.

When she faced away from him, the mounds of her buttocks jiggled enticingly under the see-through gauze of her dress, but oh, *bon Dieu*, when she turned! The bright moonlight, both from the sky and reflecting off the waves, made her creamy skin practically luminescent, and her lush body was wet and outlined perfectly by the light fabric. Even her eyes, with her thick eyelashes turned spiky by the water, seemed to glow. His breath hitched, and his body, which had still been relatively relaxed, went instantly hard again. Annelise not only made him rather poetic, it seemed, but she also made him insatiable. He didn't care, as long as he held her again…*soon*.

"What?" she asked, seeing the look on his face. "Do I have makeup running down my face? Seaweed in my hair?"

He shook his head. Not trusting himself to speak without saying something crazy, he walked slowly toward her, sloshing through the water. When he reached her, he held her gaze as he grabbed the hem of her wet dress, asking her silently for permission. The slight incline of her head was all the permission he needed, and he pulled the wet dress off her, throwing it so it landed on the sand with a wet *plop*.

He didn't pay attention to anything but Annelise. He'd thought she was lovely before, but now… He couldn't believe he'd ever thought she was normal in any way. The aqua blue of the water, dappled by the moonlight, made little circles of light all over her body and face, and she looked as if she were a part of the sea, a part of paradise. He'd been to this resort many times, with his family or alone, and he'd never thought it was as amazing as it was tonight.

He reached out to her, almost automatically, needing to feel her creamy skin, wet and cool from the water.

She parted her lips in surprise and pleasure as he smoothed caresses up and down her sides, reveling in the sensation of his warm hands against her coolness. He loved the contrast of the brown tan of his hands and arms against her pallor. He would have guessed not, but now he was almost certain that she'd probably never been outside nude, and definitely never in the sun.

"*Quelle beauté,*" he mused, slipping into French. Annelise seemed to understand him.

"You're quite gorgeous yourself, you know. Maybe it's the moonlight?" she answered, looking down quickly as if she'd surprised herself with her own bold compliment.

He, always the cynic, felt bespelled. Different. Something about her made him lighter, optimistic. He shook his head, little droplets of sea water spraying everywhere. "*Non,* the moonlight is lovely, but I think it's you and me. On this night and in this place, we're…totally in tune. As one."

He caught her warm gaze before she looked down, biting one of her full, pink lips that begged to be kissed. He realized what he'd said and laughed, the sound coming out darkly sensual.

"Aha, you perhaps like the idea of us as one?" he teased, but his cock had hardened almost painfully.

He thought he might explode right there when she looked up at him again from under her lashes and nodded. "Yes," she mouthed, at first, no sound coming out. "Yes," she repeated, more strongly, her beautiful eyes liquid with desire.

With a strangled yell, he picked her up again and cupped her bare butt, kneading the soft globes of her ass where he held it, and kissed her neck, then her chest, then up to her lips. She seemed just as ravenous as he was as she looped her arms around his neck and shoulders, pressing herself closer still until every soft part of her rubbed against him.

"Damn," he groaned, breathing heavily. "I have to put you down to take these shorts off."

Annelise slithered down his front with a sexy little shimmy, and before he even realized her intent, she knelt in the shallow, warm water and tore open his shorts. When her hot mouth closed around his hard cock, he almost shot off like a rocket, as if his earlier pleasure hadn't happened. Looking down, seeing her sucking and licking his hot, hard shaft as if it were an ice cream cone in her favorite flavor, turned him on like nothing else. He grunted with pleasure and stroked her long, damp hair. It felt too good, and if she kept going, he would never last long enough to bring her pleasure too.

When she looked up at him with a question in her eyes, her lips red and swollen, a shiver of pure lust went through him. *God damn but she is a sexy little minx.*

"You like it like that?" she asked, and her tone, husky and low, called to something inside him.

"Ah, *chérie*, if I liked it any more you'd already have my seed all over your face," he answered, pulling her to her feet.

He could tell from the way her eyes darkened that she liked his dirty talk, something he'd noticed earlier. Quickly stepping out of his shorts, he hurled them to the shore to join her cover-up before he pulled her down into the shallow water.

Her breasts floated on the surface like two sexy buoys, and the sensation of their wet skin rubbing together, totally surrounded by the salty water, was absolutely exquisite, like nothing he'd ever felt. Rémy hadn't thought he could get any harder, but he'd been wrong.

Tugging her along, he swam them with a couple of quick strokes and kicks until he lay on the sand in the shallowest water. Understanding dawned on her flushed face when he positioned her over his swollen member, which jutted straight up from the water.

"Ride me, *bébé*," he ordered, and she sank down so that he filled her to the hilt. Her pussy was a hot, silky glove, tight all around him, as if she were made for him.

When he was seated all the way in, she gave a small cry of satisfaction. He bucked his hips experimentally and she cried out again, as if the pleasure was too much to stand. *Dieu*, he loved that sound. And he loved how the motion made her generous breasts bounce, little droplets of ocean water rolling off them.

"Bring those pretty nipples down here so I can taste them," he commanded.

She leaned forward, bracing her arms on either side of his head, and he sucked one rosy tip, already hard from the combination of the breeze with the water. She tasted salty, sweet and totally delicious. He rocked her on the spike of his cock while he licked and teased her breasts, and she let her head fall back as if she couldn't hold it up anymore, her breath hitching with pleasure.

"Rémy, oh my God, it's too much," she moaned. When she wiggled her hips, he held her firmly, lifting her up and down so he was thrusting up into her, deep and hard. Her knees and his elbows splashed in the shallow water, and the droplets of saltwater made his vision blur, but he didn't care, was too far gone to really notice. Everywhere the night breeze hit moist skin, it heightened his sensations. The warmth of her pussy, tight and liquid, surrounded his dick, squeezing it, and she felt like paradise, like she was made just for him.

When he quickened his pace even more and brushed her sensitive bundle of nerves with one fingertip, she tensed and screamed her pleasure, pulsing and quivering all around him. He felt goosebumps rise all over her and heard her gasping. The feel of her release, her tiny muscles undulating and tightening around his cock, combined with the sexy-as-hell sight of her face in the moonlight, lost in the throes of her passion, was too much for him. He arched into her once more, filling her with his hot semen over and over until she collapsed on top of him, limp and spent.

They lay there, half in and half out of the water, listening to the quiet night sounds, muted by the soothing rush and roar of the ocean and the breeze through the leaves of the tropical palms. Rémy didn't think he'd ever felt more relaxed. This was not at all how he'd expected his day to go. But wow, what a change.

He'd started the day by just working on his latest book. While his brothers both had a keen interest in the family business, and even Clothilde enjoyed many aspects of it, Rémy only got involved when he had to. He much preferred his visiting teaching appointments and various research projects focusing on different aspects of social history. He'd made a niche for himself as a sought-after social historian, bringing his subjects to life for his students in his many short-term visiting professorships. The schools often offered him longer, but he liked to be free to travel and go to different research sites on a whim. And, *bon Dieu*, his family had the money to support whatever he chose to do.

So, from a quiet, isolated morning of writing, to having passionate, soul-satisfying sex on the beach in less than twelve hours… That was a new record, even for a reputed playboy such as himself. Of course, the ridiculous reputation he and his brothers cultivated was mostly a smokescreen to keep women away. Oh, sure, he enjoyed charming, beautiful women, but he also believed in love. Real love. The kind of love his parents had had. A can't-wait-to-wake-up-in-the-morning-to-see-the-face-you-loved-best-next-to-you kind of love. The leave-a-love-note-in-the-bathroom-every-weekday-for-thirty-years kind of love. The kind of love that would prompt you to buy a little slice of paradise to make your wife happy, even though you were watching her time dwindle and her eyes get a little dimmer each day. He just didn't think he'd ever find that kind of love — wasn't sure he could handle the end of it whenever it came, however it came. So he indulged with the occasional beauty, and generally played up his reputation with the press, all to avoid any serious attention from women he might actually fall in love with. Short-term romance was all he did, was all he was willing to do.

Rémy shook himself free of the memories, coming back to the present, to the warm, wonderful, generous woman he held in his arms. Such a revelation. Normally, he'd be planning exactly what to do. He was smooth but genuine — never wanting to hurt anyone — so he'd usually extricate himself very convincingly, leaving the woman feeling cherished and happy. Afterward? Well, he hoped they still felt a warm glow when they thought about him. He was up front about wanting fun, flattered them shamelessly and usually sent a tasteful, thoughtful gift after he was no longer seeing a woman. There were never any hard feelings. He prided himself on that.

With Annelise, though, he was curiously reluctant to think about goodbye. He was used to setting the terms, and the fact that she'd set them... *That must be it.* That must be why he didn't feel the same sense of lightness at being able to do whatever he wanted, never compromising.

Annelise let herself drift on a cloud of sensation. Here, in this place, alone on the Caribbean beach surrounded by water and sand and a dark sky filled with more stars than she'd ever seen at night, she could have believed she and Rémy were alone in the world. She was buck naked, right outside in front of anyone who cared to walk by, and she didn't feel embarrassed at all. No, tonight she was proud of her body. She felt like the sea goddess Rémy had compared her to, ethereal and mysterious, the mistress of her own destiny.

Her friend Marina had been right. She'd barely thought about Kyle for the past few hours, and she knew, somehow, that she'd taken an important step. He wasn't the first thing her mind went to, and she had done that with her choice to let Rémy in, to seduce him. She'd chosen that first, most important step into a new and different future. It wasn't what she'd planned, but damn, now she was excited about it. For the first time, she wasn't looking back at what should have been, but forward, at what could be.

"Thank you," she murmured, her cheek pressed against the solid muscles of his chest. She knew her voice was muffled, but she just couldn't be troubled to move right at the moment. Her body felt too darn good.

"What was that, *bébé*?" Rémy answered, stroking her hair in a way that made her scalp tingle deliciously.

"Thank you," she repeated, a little louder this time.

"It's *I* who should be thanking *you*, no? Worshiping my lovely goddess? High priest at the shrine of Anne-lise." His words were teasing, and he twisted one long strand of hair, drying now in the breeze, around his finger. She loved the way he pronounced her name, so French, like two separate words.

"Mmm," she answered. "I think you did that." She couldn't contain the sudden mirth that rose up to fill her — or maybe it was joy. She raised her head to look at him. His hair was in the water, floating around his head, and his chin was tilted down toward her. He should have looked silly, but instead he still looked ruggedly handsome, and happy. "With your devoted and zealous worship, I think you deserve a promotion. How about being a monk?"

Rémy's indignant laughter rang out in the silvery darkness. "What? After that, you can call me a monk?" He brought his hand down on one butt cheek in a stinging slap that made her yelp with surprise and...*pleasure*?

Rémy clearly noticed her reaction. "Aha, my goddess likes that," he said with satisfaction.

She pushed herself up to stand and faced away from him, looking back over her shoulder teasingly. "Uh-uh. You're a monk now. Hands to yourself, Brother Rémy."

His eyes widened and he looked as though he might protest, but then he closed his mouth and put his hands behind his head, settling in. He might be outwardly relaxed, but his gaze was anything but as he watched her. When she gave an experimental wiggle, his eyes grew dark. Predatory.

Spurred on by some imp of mischief, she did a slow spin and raised her arms above her head. "Are you awed to be in the presence of your goddess?" she said haughtily.

"You know what your presence does to me, my lady," Rémy answered, playing along.

"Good answer, and I will reward it," she teased, shaking her hips. Something both warm and sexy unfurled deep inside her at his expression. He looked rapt, as though his gaze hung on her slightest movement.

She started to sing, an old song about stars and dreams, moving slowly, and he joined in with a rich baritone as she turned and twisted and splashed in the warm water. He didn't interrupt her. He just watched her and was with her, enjoying her playfulness as well as her sensuality and so adding to it. He never took his eyes off her, as if he didn't want to miss any tiny motion. It was oddly intimate…almost more than what they'd already shared.

When they got to the end of the song, his gaze locked with hers. Intense. Glowing. And something else…something she couldn't quite figure out. The spell was suddenly broken when she heard a noise in the bushes.

With a cry, Annelise sat down in the shallow water, covering herself with her hands and her dark hair. Rémy stood in one angry motion, fury in every line of his body. A security guard emerged from the foliage at the edge of the beach. He half-covered his eyes, and his face was averted, which she appreciated deeply.

"I thought you understood, Manuel, that we were not to be disturbed for any reason." Rémy's voice wasn't loud, but it didn't need to be. It was cold and hard, and Annelise felt a shiver go up her spine at how harsh he sounded. He was completely nude, but instead of making him look vulnerable, his unabashed nudity made him look all the more dangerous.

The lines of the guard's body looked wary but determined. The set of his shoulders was also somehow worried and sad at the same time. Over her initial shock, Annelise realized that, of course, something must be very wrong.

"It's Señorita Clothilde. There's been an accident."

Chapter Four

Rémy's skin went hot, then prickly cold, and at first he didn't hear anything else Manuel said. It was as if the other man spoke from a long tunnel. Rémy could see his mouth moving and hear he was talking, but he just couldn't make sense of the words. The touch of Annelise's cool hand on his back brought him back, centering him. Dimly, he knew that he should be touched that she had overcome her modesty to walk right over to him naked in front of someone else, but, at the moment, his thoughts were consumed by his sister.

"...at the hospital now." Finally, the other man's words sank in, and he felt a hot spark of hope flare in his chest.

"Hospital," he croaked, clearing his throat. "Hospital," he repeated. "That means...she's alive? Is she—?"

Manuel saved him from voicing any other fears with a quick reply. "She's alive, señor. Hurt badly, but she has come through surgery and they are hopeful."

"Oh, *mon Dieu. Merci, bon, bon Dieu*," Rémy breathed, feeling a little of the vise that had constricted his chest loosen incrementally. "Where? How?"

"It was a car accident just outside of Montreal. That is all I heard from Señor Pierre before he had to go. He said he had tried your mobile phone many times."

"I left it at the cabana. So stupid." Rémy felt regret the likes of which he'd never known. How could he not have been there for his family when they needed him? He scrubbed his hand down his face, hard. At a small sound behind him, he spun quickly, having nearly forgotten that Annelise was there. She looked sympathetic, caring and understanding in a way that he hadn't known he needed. At the softness in her eyes, he felt his own sting.

"I'm sorry, *chérie*," he said, meaning the words but also already thinking of how to get home the fastest. He just couldn't think of anything else.

"No, *I'm* sorry, Rémy. I hope your sister recovers quickly. I'll be" — her voice grew rough with emotion — "thinking of you. Of all of you. Go be a good brother."

Rémy pulled her hand to his lips and tugged her to him. Uncaring of their audience, he kissed her once more, putting all of his passion and regret into one embrace. When he drew back, he thought he saw tears in her eyes, but she covered her face with her hair too quickly for him to be sure.

Manuel had tactfully picked up their clothes, still without ever turning toward them fully, and he tossed them to Rémy, who handed Annelise her cover-up, now crumpled and sandy.

He tugged on his shorts and turned back to her, his beautiful goddess whom it seemed he was destined to have for only a short time, after all. She had managed to get the dirty dress back on, but she looked like she was about to walk back into the water.

"Annelise," he said. She turned, her eyes still averted. "Thank you, *bébé*. Just…thank you. I must go."

"Of course," she said, and was her voice a little thick? "Good luck."

He started to walk back toward his cabana at a quick pace but couldn't resist running back to her for one last quick embrace. He knew he'd never forget her faint scent of vanilla or the feel of her soft lips on his. He turned and left, not trusting himself to say anything else, intent on getting to Clothilde.

After he had gone, Annelise went into the water all the way up to her neck. It was much more ominous to be swimming alone in the ocean on a deserted beach, and when a cloud passed over the moon, the water grew darker, almost black. Her thoughts went to every horror movie involving sharks that she'd ever seen, but she deliberately put them out of her mind. When the cloud passed, it was like a new dawn on her life — or her outlook, at least. She lay back and floated in the water, feeling the wet, light fabric brushing over her still-sensitized nipples. That morning — heck, that afternoon even — she'd still been holding on to the past, trapped by it. But now, with her impulsive offer to Rémy, she'd come alive again. And his emergency and abrupt departure had been a stark reminder of how fragile life could be. She prayed that his sister, who'd had so much heartache herself and betrayal even deeper than Annelise's, would recover. She realized that she'd never know, and the thought made her sad. And yet, she and Rémy would have had to part eventually anyway, so maybe at least his quick, clean departure was a blessing.

Certainly, she was done with her grief. Exactly as her friend had said, she'd given several years of her life to Kyle and she wasn't letting him have another minute, not one second. Wonderful people, like Rémy, were out there just waiting for her. Her friends, those patient, understanding souls, like Marina, were just standing by to give her space or fun or whatever she needed. They stood by each other. She'd been letting herself drift a little at work lately, too. Oh, not doing a bad job, but not doing much more than she had to. She'd lost her zeal and enthusiasm. That stopped right now. This instant.

When she paddled back to the shallow water where she and Rémy had so recently made wild, wonderful love and she stood up, wringing out her hair, she felt a pang of sadness which she promptly quashed. *Nope.* That beautiful man had been her choice, hers for one night, and in those moments, she'd been his, too. That would be enough. It had to be.

As if to punctuate her thoughts, she heard the thwap-thwap of rotors approaching then leaving quickly too, all while she walked in from the water and up toward her cabana.

* * * *

Six months later

It was cold...freezing cold, so the tips of her fingers went numb even inside her thick gloves. But she should have expected that. The entire country of Canada was north of Massachusetts, Maine and Minnesota, so why wouldn't it be frigid? It was November, for heaven's sake! She just hadn't been prepared for the bone-chilling wind that took her breath away. She loved it, though, every cobblestone and iron lamppost. The streets of Montreal were charming, the architecture a blend of European and North American tastes. And the people were incredibly friendly, warm and vibrant. It was as if they tried to offset the harsh climate by being as kind and generous as the wind was cold. She hadn't met a single truly ill-tempered person in the week that she'd been there already.

If she had occasionally thought she'd seen a familiar, tall silhouette and a wide grin, well, that was nobody's business but her own. She was there for work and nothing else. Work that was, incidentally, going extremely well. Her firm was considering opening an office in Montreal, based on all the new work that they'd been getting, and the series of meetings and events she'd set up had gotten even more of a positive response than she'd expected. Since she'd gotten back from that life-changing Caribbean trip, she had been working hard and it had paid off. These ten days of coordination in Montreal were a way for her to prove she deserved the promotion she thought was very likely going to be offered when she returned.

Without exaggeration or false pride, she knew she was an excellent administrative and event coordinator for her financial services firm, but she also knew she'd be a superlative client relationship manager. No more managing calendars, no more tactful communications on behalf of her boss… The promotion would be a step into an entirely new phase of her career. She would be able to prove herself in her own right and, hopefully, continue right on up the chain to a director or even vice president position. As soon as Charles, her boss and mentor for the past five years, had mentioned this trip and today's meetings and evening event in particular, she'd known it was a turning point. High-profile and demanding, chock full of client relationship-building and new business opportunities, this trip to Montreal was her perfect proving ground.

When Charles had told her the location, she'd felt a twinge of discomfort. She was taking a break from men for a little while, and while she had no regrets about her time with Rémy, she still thought about him more than she wanted to. To go to his city… It felt funny. Then her common sense had kicked in. It was a huge city. Enormous. The second-largest French-speaking city in the world. The odds that she'd run into the one person she'd rather not see were astronomical. And even if she did see him? Well then, she'd be fine. She'd gotten over the funny ache she would sometimes get in the very center of her chest when she thought of him, and she could get over it again if she had to — which she wouldn't, because she wouldn't see him.

Now that she was here, she was grateful she'd overcome her reservations. It was the professional opportunity of a lifetime, and she was now focused on success and having fun with her friends. Since she'd returned from Mexico, she'd been dedicated and genuinely engaged, both professionally and personally. Every time a friend called for drinks or a party, she went and had a great time. She worked long hours, volunteering for committees and special projects, from the initiative on streamlining meetings to the fall school supply drive, and she contributed meaningfully. She was in a great place, personally and career-wise, and she loved to see all her careful event-planning and organization yield flawlessly-executed events.

She was walking — well, trotting might be a more apt term, given how darn cold it was — to the hotel venue for today's series of meetings and the subsequent cocktail reception her firm was hosting that evening. She knew it was close. She'd taken a cab several days earlier and it had hardly pulled away from the curb before it had pulled over, but goodness, what felt close in a car felt like a long way in high-heeled boots in the snow. She'd wanted to make sure today's scheduled events were extra perfect. Okay, it wasn't possible to be better than perfect. But…if it were, this was the time to pull off that superhuman feat.

Today's meetings, along with tonight's reception, were for her division's biggest client, Gaspard Industries, headed by some sort of dynastic family that was a Very Big Deal in Montreal. Well, actually in all of Quebec and beyond. The only wrinkle was that unfortunately the scion and CEO, Pierre, had been called away urgently the previous week and one of the other family members — another brother, she thought — was going to attend everything in his place. She hoped she'd impress him and, thus, her company would impress him, as much as they apparently had Pierre, who was generally very satisfied with their work.

When she got into the lobby, she had to stamp her feet briskly a few times, partly to get rid of the slushy snow and partly to get feeling back into her toes. As she waited to warm up enough so she wouldn't do something so totally unprofessional as shivering, she looked around slowly. She'd reviewed a wide variety of pictures, of course, that Marie, the senior conference and event coordinator at the hotel, had emailed as part of the proposal, but her prior site visit several days earlier had been rushed and she'd only really looked at the conference rooms and ballroom where her events would be held. Now, she realized that the pictures hadn't done this gorgeous lobby justice. She felt like she was stepping back in time, right into Montreal's Edwardian heyday of opulence and tasteful elegance. Someone had done an exquisite job restoring the structure, though it must cost a fortune to maintain. She felt a warm glow of satisfaction, mentally congratulating herself on having chosen what must be the best possible venue for these meetings.

It was important that she and Charles and the small team of senior analysts, all hand-picked by her boss, conveyed their understanding of, and appreciation for, the important history of Gaspard Industries and the other large, established Quebecois businesses they were meeting with. Gaspard Industries and Montreal were closely linked, so having multiple meetings in such a superb historical location that also had tasteful modern touches seemed ideal.

Nodding again, she smiled without thinking. Then she broke into a full smile. *Why shouldn't I be happy?* With everything coming together so well, what could possibly happen to stand in the way of her promotion? She hurried to the coat room, leaving her coat and larger bag with the attendant, and went to check on the status of the setup of the breakfast spread in the smaller conference room, where the morning's first meeting was to take place.

The *Salle Cartier*, nicely also labeled with small letters underneath that said *Cartier Room*, was almost cozy, with cream-colored printed wallpaper that looked like it might be silk. The small crystal chandelier, though, above the enormous boardroom table that she'd been assured would comfortably seat fourteen to sixteen people kept up the same level of elegance that the lobby had possessed. To her relief, she saw there was a table set in the small antechamber which held an array of scrumptious-looking breakfast items, currently covered to protect their freshness, all displayed in what appeared to be an enormous silver service that would have been right at home on the table in a ballroom in one of the Edwardian mansions she'd driven past several times now as she went to various locations in Montreal.

Again, she felt the same deep satisfaction of a job well done, which changed to dismay in an instant when she realized what she didn't see in the room — the projector and screen she'd specifically requested. She spun on her heel and nearly ran over the petite, stylish older woman, Marie, with whom she'd been working on all of the arrangements.

The greeting died on the other woman's lips at the expression on Annelise's face.

"I was going to ask if everything was to your satisfaction, but I can see that *non*, something is not right." She was professional and her tone conveyed both an unspoken apology as well as an understanding of the importance to Annelise. As a fellow coordinator, Annelise was impressed.

"It looks like we're missing the projector and screen, and I'd hoped to test running this morning's presentation from my laptop," Annelise explained. She wasn't happy, but she knew from years of experience that something almost always went awry at the last minute. That was why she was here almost an hour early, to smooth out whatever unknown issue had cropped up.

Marie shook her head, clucking, which made her sharp, dark bob shake as well, almost as if it were also disappointed. "I will go to fix this immediately." And she strode off with purpose.

The screen arrived quickly, but the projector took longer, and Annelise checked the time on her cell phone several times. She tested the presentation again on her laptop, and all of the video portions were still running well, so she wasn't too worried that it looked like she wasn't going to be able to run her usual test. She refused to even begin to panic. Everything would work out in the end. But, *argh*, it was frustrating. She could sense Marie's rising frustration, too, as the woman had returned several times with status updates. Apparently the projector had been set up in the wrong room but that group had already begun with it right in the center of their table, so removal had been more of a delicate operation.

Finally, a scant ten minutes before the meeting was scheduled to start, a sheepish-looking young man with dark-rimmed glasses rolled in the projector.

"Awesome! Boy, am I glad to see you!" She flashed him a grateful smile.

"Again, so sorry about the mix-up." He spoke with a soft accent.

She waved away his apology.

"Totally appreciate it, but I think we're going to be fine. Let's just get it set up as quickly as we can. I'm happy to help." She understood. She genuinely did. And, frankly, she didn't have time to be difficult, even if she'd wanted to be.

He nodded and started to put the projector in place, screwing and plugging in all of the necessary cables rapidly then adjusting the bottom height screws to make sure the picture would project at the right height.

"Here... I can run these under the table," she offered, eyeing the setup. It was a lovely table, but she knew it must be hiding its tech somewhere. "Are the plug-ins in the center?" she guessed.

"*Oui*, yes. Right there," he answered, gesturing to where she'd thought made the most sense. A pain, since it looked to be right under the middle of the giant table, but normally these things were already in place prior to meetings. She nodded and took the sound, VG and power cables, dropping to her knees in spite of how it made the skirt of her suit ride up a little—thankfully, no one was here yet—and crawling with the wires so they would be hidden entirely under the table. She'd done this sort of thing countless times before at other events, but she was cutting it pretty darn close on this one. She fumbled a bit and had to take out her phone to use as a flashlight to get the last cord hooked up. She heard a muffled voice, which she thought was the IT guy making his exit, though she couldn't be sure.

As she scrambled to back out the side of the table, which she realized belatedly was actually the side that faced the door instead of the windows, two thoughts registered at once. First, that she felt a breeze much higher up on the backs of her thighs than she was comfortable with, but, worse than that, the breeze meant someone had just opened the door. Praying that it was Marie coming back—or even the IT guy—she instead heard the voice she was dreading. Charles, her boss. Her stomach lurched.

"Happy to get to know you better, and please give Pierre our best as well, of course. Our event coordinator, who I'm also lucky enough to have as an assistant, should be around here somewhere."

At his words, all hope she'd still held that he might be alone faded. She had a split second to debate whether to crawl all the way through, but someone in the group likely had seen her already, or, at least, one part of her. They *had* to have been able to. The room just wasn't that big. Maybe they wouldn't notice if she stayed totally still? While she was still hesitating, another voice spoke.

"Er, perhaps she's the woman I saw in the lobby. Young, with a gray skirt and black boots?"

The familiar timbre—deep and gravelly, with the hint of an accent—froze her, and her stomach felt like it might fall right out of her body onto the floor. It couldn't be *him, could it*? No, it *must* be someone else. There was no way that the one man in Montreal who was currently, by the volume and direction of his voice, able to see almost all the way to the bottom of her lucky black lace panties was her mysterious lover from Mexico.

"Ah, that does sound like her. If you'll excuse me, Remington?" Charles' voice was already getting quieter, as he must be walking to the door.

Remington? Could Rémy be short for…Remington? *Holy freaking cow. How is it possible that the universe hates me this much?* She groaned.

"The coast is clear. You can come out now."

His voice, even closer now, like he was bending over a little, made her jump and half sit up—well, as much as she could—smacking her head on the thick wood of the table with a thud that seemed to echo from her temples to her nose. Or maybe that was just the sound of her embarrassment being compounded more than she'd thought possible.

"*Oh la*, are you all right? Let me help you."

Then somehow, she wasn't sure exactly, she'd been pulled back onto her feet and was leaning on the conference table, staring at a face she'd never expected to see again in person. The face, with those dark, sparkling eyes, and easy smile, had lived in her dreams for months. Rémy was *here*.

Her mouth fell open with surprise. Her heart and stomach fluttered. She'd thought maybe her memory had exaggerated how handsome he'd been, but if anything, her memories hadn't done him justice. His face was still like a sculpture of a Renaissance warrior, with a distinguished nose, strong chin and lips that she knew were incongruously soft. Now, though, instead of faded shorts, he wore a suit that must have been tailored to fit him so perfectly. In fact, he looked...polished. Smooth. The complete opposite of the man she remembered. But after all, she'd only known him very briefly.

At first, he looked as stunned as she felt. Frozen. Then he collected himself. "Annelise," he said, his voice low and intimate, and instantly the changes to his appearance didn't matter. He sounded exactly the same, with that rich, beautiful voice. Her name as two smooth words. She felt goosebumps rise on her arms, even through her suit coat. "I should have known two such perfect asses could never have been created."

She was torn between shock and laughter at his words, but when he waggled his eyebrows suggestively in a gesture she remembered from their time together, she had to turn her laugh into a cough.

God, he's charming. And handsome. And apparently...a client? That thought sobered her right away.

"Nice to meet you, *Monsieur Gaspard*," she answered, proud of how steady and unaffected her voice sounded. She held out her hand, but Rémy pointedly didn't take it, taking a step closer instead until she withdrew it.

"You look wonderful, *bébé*. I have thought of you..."

Whatever he was going to say — and darn it, client or not, she wished she'd gotten to hear it — was cut off by the hearty voice of her boss. "Trust you to find the VIP and charm him before I've even had a chance to properly introduce you, Annelise! I must have just missed you in the lobby. Remington, this is my assistant, Annelise Simpkins." Charles gestured cordially toward her with one perfectly groomed hand.

"Remington," she echoed, but she knew her smile was weak.

Charles shot her a surprised look, which he quickly hid. It wasn't like her not to immediately flash a thousand-watt smile and offer to take care of...something, and she knew that he'd picked up on the vibe between them.

She took a deep breath and gave herself a split-second internal pep talk. She was confident, she was cool under pressure and she was a future major client relationship manager. By God, she could act like it! Letting out the breath, she hurried to cover up her gaffe.

"Monsieur Gaspard, *Remington*," she repeated more heartily, and extended her hand again. "What a pleasure to meet you. We're so happy you could come."

Rémy took her hand in both of his and she barely covered a gasp. The gesture felt so familiar that it made her chest ache. When he held it to his lips briefly, she felt a spark of heat and excitement that she hadn't felt in months, since she'd last seen him.

"*Enchanté*," he murmured, and while there was nothing overly familiar about the gesture, which she'd learned was actually not uncommon in Montreal, the teasing sparkle in his eyes was intimate, as if they shared a private jest. Which, she supposed, they did.

She smiled again, knowing it was over-bright but unable to tone it down, and she gave a little wave toward the food table, where the pastries were now uncovered and waiting to be enjoyed.

"Please help yourselves. There's coffee and other breakfast items, and the others should be arriving any moment now."

"Thanks," Charles answered, shooting her his boyishly charming grin, the one she thought might have made a lot of female hearts flutter thirty years earlier, then her boss turned toward Rémy. "Annelise always makes sure we have great food and drinks at meetings. It helps keep everyone comfortable. Shall we?"

Rémy nodded, and the two men began to shuffle over to the table, but then he half-turned back. "Can I get you a coffee, too? Ms., er...Simpkins?"

She was warmed to her core, even as she regretted how his actions were drawing unwelcome attention from Charles. Rémy obviously didn't know how these things worked—that no one, especially not an executive or client, ever offered her coffee at a meeting. It just wasn't done...except by him.

When he caught her gaze, his was dark with...something, something she couldn't read. And suddenly she thought that maybe he did know how these things usually worked after all.

She gave her head a little shake and had to look away from the intensity of his look. "No, thank you. I'll just be here another moment then I'll get out of your way!"

The sounds behind her made it clear that they'd gone to the breakfast table and that a couple of the analysts had arrived, as she finished firing up the projector, which seemed to be working perfectly now. But she could have sworn she actually felt the heat of Rémy's glances on her back several times. She was grateful when it was time that she could finally escape, unobtrusively. Usually Charles didn't even notice when she left. Rémy, on the other hand, turned at the last moment before she could quietly close the door, his dark eyes focused entirely on her. Hot and full of promise, the look made her shiver, which was utterly inappropriate for a business meeting. She raised her chin and glared in return before she allowed the door to swish closed with barely a sound.

She hurried to the next, larger conference room where this afternoon's meetings were to be held. She'd slip back into the Cartier Room in a little while, just to be sure everything was still going smoothly, and, of course, Charles wouldn't hesitate to text her about any issues, but in the meantime, she wanted to check that the *Salle Groseilliers* was set up correctly. And she wanted a moment to collect herself. As she passed in front of the mirrored panels in part of the lobby, cloudy with age but still glorious, she caught sight of her ass. And damned if it didn't look great in her skirt. She shook her head with a smile, covering another snort of amusement.

Rémy sipped his coffee and watched the beginning of the morning's presentation as if he were following it, but his mind was occupied elsewhere. Seeing Annelise, even though he'd been forewarned and, he'd thought, prepared, had still been a shock. *Bon Dieu*, but she was breathtaking. An unwilling smile tugged at his lips as he recalled her position when he'd walked in, but he firmly told himself to remain objective. He'd assured his brothers and sister, as well as the head of their private security team, that he could do this. He'd suggested it, in fact. But he hadn't bargained on how much seeing her would affect him. He tapped his pen on his lip absently and smiled vaguely at whatever joke the presenter had obviously just made.

No matter how strongly he still felt a pull toward her, he needed to focus on their plan. He would bide his time, waiting for the right opportunity, then he would give Charles the information. They'd used similar tactics with several other people linked to various companies that might be connected, but to no avail. In all likelihood, this would come to nothing as well. In light of recent events, though, they just couldn't afford to discount any possibilities, no matter how remote. Until he knew for certain, he needed to keep his eye on the prize and not his beautiful sea goddess. He acknowledged, if only to himself, that he was eager to cross Annelise and her company off their list of potentially suspicious entities. Once he did, there wasn't anything standing in the way of him pursuing her in a different way, and now that he'd seen her and spoken with her again, he found he was surprised at how much he wanted to pick up right where they'd left off.

Chapter Five

Everything seemed to be in place in the next room, but when she peeked into the ballroom, she saw that a few of the taller café-height tables and chairs she'd wanted around the perimeter weren't quite where she wanted them. Marie, who'd stopped by to check in again on how everything was going, said she'd be more than happy to move them and grabbed a couple of the conference-setup hotel staff. Annelise thought they'd gotten everything in place to her satisfaction, and she checked the time on her cell phone again, pleased that it looked like they'd be able to finish up before she went back to the first room to touch base with Charles over their first scheduled break.

As she was about to tell everyone that she was happy with the changes, the three young men who'd been helping her stilled and went silent, looking at something behind her. Some*one*. With a sinking feeling, and knowing she would be right, she turned to see Rémy standing in the doorway, looking devastatingly handsome, as always. His tall frame was lit from behind as he was framed by the gilded doors, and he looked almost like an angel. Well, if angels were the stuff of women's fantasies.

When she would have nonchalantly turned back to work, trying to pretend he wasn't there, he said something to the three young men that sent them practically running from the room. She wished, not for the first time, that her French was better, although she'd always found the distinctive Quebecois accent a little bit harder to understand when she'd taken French in high school. '*As different from a Parisian accent as a Scotsman's was from someone from Alabama,*' her teacher had quipped.

"I can't believe... How did you do that?" she demanded in a low voice, glaring at him. In the large empty space, even a quiet sound carried perfectly.

Rémy raised an eyebrow and her stomach gave an involuntary flip. *Goodness but he's charming. He doesn't even have to open his mouth.*

"I simply asked for them to excuse us. I own this hotel—or, rather, my family does. But they know who I am, so..." He shrugged as if to say that it was just a foregone conclusion that everyone would jump to do his bidding. An image of the security guard, Manuel, on the beach, speaking so deferentially to Rémy sprang to mind. Maybe that was exactly what he was used to. When she looked up, the errant thought that he was watching her reaction carefully flew through her head, but his expression changed and she thought she'd imagined it.

"So, you're some kind of...tycoon?" she asked, feeling somehow as if he had lied to her, even though they hadn't exactly exchanged addresses and agreed to be pen pals. "Wait! Your family owns the cabanas, too, don't they?" She couldn't believe it hadn't even occurred to her until this moment, especially since he'd told her he was occupying the owner's cabana.

Rémy stepped closer to her, walking until he was only a foot or so from her while she stood, unmoving. He gave her every opportunity to move away, and she knew she ought to maintain a professional distance now that she knew who he was. But she didn't want to. Not right this moment, anyway. His smile was one of satisfaction.

"First, *chérie*, I don't believe anyone uses the term 'tycoon' anymore."

"You know what I mean," she huffed.

"Yes, then I suppose you could call my family 'tycoons'. Or my brother a 'magnate'. 'Leaders of industry'?"

"You're making fun of me."

Rémy's expression, which had been light, grew very serious. "Never, Annelise. Fun, yes, but never to make you feel silly."

He reached out one large hand, brushing it gently against her hair and cheek. His movements were slow, almost as if he expected her to flee at any moment, like a startled doe.

"You look even better than I remember, and, *chérie*, my memories of that night are pretty fantastic."

Annelise wanted to disagree, but he was echoing her own thoughts.

"I'm sorry I didn't tell you who I was. We introduced ourselves and… Well, we just didn't talk about anything like that, *bébé*."

She sighed and bit her lip. "No, we didn't," she conceded. And really, she couldn't be angry with him in good conscience. Everything about that night had been disconnected from the normal and the everyday. "But now that we know, anything like...well, *this*" — she motioned between them, nearly hitting his chest — "is totally inappropriate."

Rémy didn't look perturbed. In fact, he raised one dark eyebrow and looked...*amused*?

"*Chérie*, it's not as though I tore that sexy little suit off you and pushed you up against the wall so I could sink balls deep into your sweet little pussy."

Her gasp was loud in the enormous space, and her face flushed. She couldn't have said what part of the heat that coursed through her suddenly was arousal at the image his words conjured and what part was indignation, but she suspected arousal might have been the winner. Before she could sputter out her reply, he continued.

"And I'm not your client, not really. I'm only standing in for Pierre until he returns. I don't generally have much to do with the family business these days, not anymore — unless there's an emergency. Then they dust me off and trot me out." Something in his voice made her think there was more to it than that — or at least more to the history — but she tamped down her curiosity.

"You're enough of a client that it is wildly inappropriate." She put her hands on her hips and straightened her spine, although she still had to look up to see his face, even in her high-heeled boots. "If Charles even suspected —" She sucked in a quick breath as another thought occurred to her. "Why are you here now? It isn't quite break time."

"I had to step out to make an urgent call, so we decided to take an earlier break."

She blew out a large breath, making her hair tickle her face, her mind already racing with what she was supposed to confirm during the break. "I have to go. But I'm glad we understand each other. No matter how sexy you are or how amazing we are together..." She trailed off as she realized what she was saying. "I mean, um..."

Rémy's chuckle was both sensual and amused. "So, you still think I'm sexy, eh?"

Annelise wanted to refute it, because it didn't really matter that she still thought he was possibly the hottest man she'd ever seen, but...she was almost incurably honest, so why stop now?

"You must know that I do. But, Rémy, my having a relationship with a client would be wrong. Now, I really do have to go." She turned to leave, but looked back at him, already wondering how in the world she was walking away.

He nodded. "Of course, *bébé*. A relationship with a client would be totally wrong. I understand."

Okay, then. Why did she feel curiously deflated by his easy agreement?

He leaned closer again, so she could feel the warmth radiating from him, and whispered, "If you look up the org chart on the website for Gaspard Industries, I think you'll find that my name isn't on it anywhere." He straightened and gave a wolfish smile. "I trust I'll see you later?"

She nodded and hurried out of the ballroom, the tapping of her heels echoing in the large space. She tried to ignore the feeling that she might be escaping as much as hurrying to check in with her boss.

* * * *

Following the afternoon meetings, when Annelise was briefly back at her hotel to get ready for the evening, she glanced at the in-room digital clock and allowed herself the luxury of flopping backward onto the bed with a groan. She'd kicked off her boots, temporarily, as soon as she'd crossed the threshold to her room, even before the door had fully shut.

Man, oh, man, were her feet tired after a day of running around the hotel. She groaned again, remembering that she'd be in heels all evening too. But this was what she wanted. This was a dress rehearsal for all the events she'd attend in the future in her dream job, especially if she did eventually make it to vice president, which she fully intended to. She really enjoyed Charles. He'd been patient with her since her first day, always explaining the reasoning behind decisions so she could have better tools to think through issues herself. He was a large part of the reason she enjoyed her work so much and why she'd been so successful. She respected and liked him enormously, even while he had his foibles. Everyone did, after all.

Luckily, the rest of the afternoon had gone smoothly, with only a little hiccup when the afternoon coffee had come without the soy milk she'd specifically requested. Still, she'd felt safe heading back to her hotel to rest for a scant half-hour or so before she'd have to get ready for the evening event. She'd almost been tempted to stay to oversee the rest of the setup in the ballroom, but she'd told herself that she'd have a chance to look the food over at the event itself. Of course, a small part of her brain had whispered that maybe she'd just wanted to be sure she looked good before she saw Rémy again, but she pointedly ignored that whisper.

Even though she tried to relax, her brain refused to slow. If anything, with the quiet and finally freed of distractions, her mind replayed their earlier interactions. He'd looked amazing, naturally, but even more, he was just as funny and sweet as she'd remembered. Smart and irreverent, though now he was wrapped in a business suit instead of a bathing suit, he still made her heartbeat speed up and her whole body tingle. And it seemed like he might still feel the same pull toward her, too.

Sighing again, she rolled to her side, tracing a pattern on the white coverlet with one finger, considering. She wasn't wavering on her relationship hiatus. She definitely still needed a long break from anything serious. In fact, she wasn't sure she would ever want that again, certainly not what she'd had with Kyle. In retrospect, with the clarity brought on by overcoming her sadness, she could see that she'd always been compromising, ceding, making sure he was happy, even if it made her unhappy. If she ever loved again, she would have to find someone incredibly special, a true partner and someone who was as supportive of her career and success as she would be of his. She thought she might be okay, too, on her own if she never found the man who could be that. The devastation she'd felt after her break-up with Kyle and, more importantly, her recovery, had taught her that she was even stronger than she'd realized. When faced with herself, stripped down, she'd understood that, above all, she needed to be someone she liked. And she'd focused on just being that person until she was certain that she truly liked herself. She would have to like anyone else she was with just as much—no compromises.

As it had all afternoon, that secret voice in her head, the sassy one who sounded a lot like her best friend, reminded her that she didn't have to pursue a relationship with Rémy to enjoy him. And if she could see her way clear to agreeing that he wasn't a real client? Well, then... She had looked up the organizational chart for Gaspard Industries, and just as he'd suggested, while his two brothers and sister were all there in various roles, his name had been totally absent. She would have been lying if she'd said she hadn't dreamed of being with him again, feeling his warm skin against hers, his hardness pressed all along her softness, him moving deep inside her, filling her. Nothing had ever felt better or brought her more pleasure. And he'd seemed to feel the same way. Still undecided, but considering, she reluctantly rolled off the bed, planting her feet on the plush hotel carpet, and padded into the bathroom to get ready for the evening ahead. At the very least, it promised not to be another dull event.

* * * *

Rémy frowned at what his older brother on the other end of the line was telling him. Scowled, really. He'd paused halfway into donning his tuxedo, so he wore his pants with his shirt untucked and only one gold cufflink done up. He held the phone with his other hand.

"They took *nothing*?"

"Not that we've found. I'm reviewing the video feeds with Villiers. *Merde*, I wish he or Marc had stayed hidden at the house instead." Rémy could picture Pierre's expression. His brother had been the acting head of their family since he was in his late teens, and the head of a multi-billion-dollar business empire since he was just over twenty. Not getting what he wanted was something he had a distinct lack of experience with. They all did. Pierre was pissed off.

Rémy sighed, feeling distinctly frustrated himself. "It made the most sense for Villiers to be with you and for Marc to be with Clothilde. Your safety is a top priority, especially since we're not sure which one of you is in the most danger. Plus, this seemed like the least likely lead that we had."

"Yeah, you're right. It's just... Whoever did this was a real pro. And it's brazen to break into a house like ours in broad daylight without leaving a trace. They were looking for something or leaving something that we haven't found yet. I'm sorry, *mon grand*, but you know what this means."

They were both silent as they considered the implications, and Rémy sat down heavily on the edge of his bed.

"*Oui*. Pinkston or someone else from his company is connected to these attacks. He told someone the information I gave him and only him." They'd thought it was the perfect bait to dangle, since normally Pierre, Clothilde, a number of staff members and often Rémy himself would have been home that day. It had certainly proven irresistible to someone.

"You're certain no one overheard?" Pierre asked. Rémy appreciated that his brother wasn't jumping to quick conclusions, but that wasn't Pierre's way.

He thought back and shook his head, even though Pierre couldn't see him. "Positive. I made sure of it. And Marc swept the room for bugs first thing this morning. It was Pinkston." Rémy hated that the hope he'd held out that no one from Annelise's company was involved was slipping away to nothing. Someone *had* to be involved. There was no other explanation.

"Marc and Villiers knew, too," Pierre said.

Rémy knew Pierre was playing devil's advocate, making them consider every possibility before proceeding along a course that his brother knew he would find distasteful. Wrong, even.

"I know what you're doing, *mon frère*. It's not them. Villiers has been our head of security for years. You were in his wedding, and you're the godfather to one of his children. And Marc had impeccable references. He passed every background check with flying colors, including your no-bullshit meter. No, they have to be connected. I just don't understand how...or why." Rémy twisted his one cufflink absently, watching the light glint off of the carved gold.

"*Bien*, well...are you still on board with our plan, then?"

Rémy grunted. It had been so easy to talk about in the abstract when he hadn't really expected this development. In fact, he'd thought it had been more about him wanting to see Annelise again, as opposed to letting his brother Luc spend time with her. Now, it was all too real. *Merde, alors.*

"Was that a yes?" his brother finally asked.

"Yes. I said I would do this and I will." Rémy could hear the reluctance in his own voice, but...if Pierre wanted blind obedience, he could call one of his thousands of lackeys instead. Realizing he was royally pissed in general and being somewhat unfair, Rémy took a deep breath. "How are you feeling? How's Clothilde? Is she really up to coming tonight?"

"I'm fine," Pierre said gruffly, which meant that he wasn't really that fine, especially since he refused to take the pain pills that the doctor prescribed. "Clothilde is having an okay day. She's still against our plan. I believe her exact words were that we were idiots and cretins, so she's definitely coming. In fact, I already had to talk Luc out of rushing back from Paris again, too. But he understands we need him there, following up on leads and taking care of all the business that has to happen to run a huge part of the company."

Rémy smiled. Their younger brother could be as impetuous as Pierre was deliberate, but only when it came to his personal life. He understood business with a skill that was nearly genius, and in that realm, he could always be reasoned with.

"Thanks for that. Okay, well, let me know if you find anything more on the video feeds, and otherwise, I'll check in when I have more info."

"Sounds good," Pierre answered.

"Oh, and try to stay safe, eh?" Rémy teased, but there was an underlying serious tone, too.

"Always," Pierre quipped. "You too." And the call disconnected.

Rémy sat there, unmoving, for a moment longer. *Can Annelise be a part of this?* Once the question popped into his mind, he couldn't discard it. He mentally turned the question over and over, not wanting to even consider it, but realizing he had to. Now that he'd thought of it, with the probable connection to her company revealed, she seemed the most likely common link. How had he never made the connection before? He'd practically just left Clothilde's side when he'd gone to Mexico and met Annelise. He'd been captivated by her and totally drawn in by the time she'd stumbled over him. It had felt natural and, damn it, he wanted to believe it had *been* natural, but it was truly incredible that, after their affair in Mexico had ended so abruptly and with no information exchanged, he would see her here in Montreal, to have his family's business be a client of her firm. The image of her crawling under the table when he'd first seen her this morning that had so amused him at the time now took on a sinister slant. Had she been placing a bug that they'd missed? And had she placed one in the afternoon conference room, too?

The bigger secret—the one only his family and several security advisors knew—was that Clothilde's accident hadn't been an accident at all. She *had* been in a car accident, yes, but her vehicle had been skillfully tampered with. If Villiers hadn't had a forensic mechanic connection, they might never have known that it wasn't just a defect with her car. It would have been ruled a tragic stroke of bad luck but nobody's fault. Thanks to that careful examination, though, they'd discovered that it had been an attempt to murder her—or possibly Pierre. They couldn't discount that possibility since Clothilde had been using a car that Pierre often favored. If someone knew the family well—and they must—they would know that Pierre or Clothilde would be equally likely to choose the sleek high-performance luxury car. Luc favored his sports car, when he wasn't in Europe as he had been so often since deciding to head up operations there, and Rémy favored his Jeep. That had been a major stumbling block in figuring out a motive. Without a clear idea of which of his siblings had been the actual target, they'd kept spinning their wheels. But if Annelise and her company had inside information somehow and had known for a fact that it would be Clothilde, that would change things drastically.

Things had escalated recently, with several more insidious attacks. Most of them had been noticed and prevented by Villiers or Marc in advance, but then, just two weeks earlier, Pierre had gotten suddenly, violently ill, poisoned by coffee brought to him at his favorite restaurant after finishing dinner with Clothilde and Rémy. Each of their coffees had been poisoned, analysis in a private lab revealed, but Pierre had taken the first sip. That was when they'd put out the story that Pierre had had to travel out of town suddenly, but really, he'd needed to recover. However, they hadn't wanted to let the attacker know how close he'd come, and they'd started trying to draw him out—or her, Rémy corrected himself. *Him or her.* He needed to remember that the attacker could be a woman.

The cynical part of him, the one that had had countless women throw themselves at him, was resigned to believing the worst, had maybe almost been waiting for it. He just truly hadn't expected it from her. But the rest of him—the real man, underneath the image and the defenses—refused that theory. *No.* Annelise might be part of something... In fact, with how he'd given the information only to Charles Pinkston, it was nearly impossible that she wasn't somehow involved, but she could be an unwitting player. She hadn't been acting with him. He would have known. He'd learned the hard way to recognize artifice, fake affection, even fake lovemaking. Their connection, her sorrow, even her unbridled passion... Those had been real. He believed that. And yet the very explosive nature of their connection—the way it drew him in like almost nothing else could—made him more suspicious. She could almost have been created as a perfect distraction for him. But if she *were* a distraction, what was the endgame?

He thought of a dozen different theories but discarded them just as quickly. None of them quite fit. But now, knowing that she was part of it…even unconsciously…he knew what he had to do, what Pierre had reminded him of. His duty was to his family, first and always. He needed to use his connection to Annelise to get information. He wanted to learn about her company, her boss, how they felt about Pierre and any other connections. The best way to do that was to pump her for information when her defenses were down. He would continue his plan to seduce her, but now it took on a whole different meaning.

Even as he steeled himself for the evening ahead, he felt a curious tightness in the back of his throat. If his instincts were totally off and she *was* somehow involved, then screw her. She deserved it. But if she wasn't—and almost everything in him told him that she must be an unconscious pawn—then she wouldn't forgive him when she found out he'd been using her. He would be throwing away the first genuine connection with a woman that he'd ever felt. It shouldn't have mattered so much, and yet, it did. He stood and drew himself up to his full height, pushing away the tightness and instead focusing on what his sister had looked like, small and pale in her hospital bed—nearly dead, but for a stroke of luck—remembering the horrible feeling of helplessness as Pierre had gone pale and sweaty after an otherwise nice family dinner before they'd rushed him to the emergency room.

Rémy would do what had to be done, just as he always had.

Chapter Six

Returning to the hotel that evening, Annelise decided to take a cab. It was extravagant, since she would feel silly expensing something like that, but darn it, it got *cold* in this city. After dark, the cold could slice right through her coat and straight to her bones. She should have brought out the heavy artillery—heck, a down coat, hat, muffler and maybe even snow pants wouldn't have been amiss—but that would have ruined the semblance of a figure that she still retained with just her woolen overcoat. *Ah, vanity.* And...she hadn't brought her heavy coat. So, a cab was a must.

In spite of avoiding most of the cold walk, even just the walk from the taxi to the hotel's front doors was enough to make her breathless, and her cheeks stung where she'd briefly left them exposed to the wind. She'd also managed to get icy slush on her boots, which she was stamping off as she entered looking down so she didn't notice that she was on a collision course with a large, familiar form.

She bumped into him with enough force that she might have stumbled or even fallen, except strong hands shot out to hold her shoulders, steadying her. Mortified, she looked up, certain whose face she would see. Because…why would something like this happen to her with anyone else? Sure enough, Rémy's dark glare looked back at her, gleaming. She noticed right away that something seemed different. There was a certain tightness around his eyes and mouth that hadn't been there before. She worried that she'd managed to really hurt him somehow before he'd caught her.

"Are you all right?" he asked, more conversationally than she could have managed at the moment.

She nodded, clearing her throat to test whether her voice would work.

"And you?"

"I'm fine," he answered, but his tone was clipped.

She frowned and was about to ask again when she saw Charles, striking in a tux with his silver hair combed back from his face, hurrying up behind Rémy.

"Ah, perfect, Annelise!" After five years, she understood that Charles, who was not only charming and sophisticated but also quite a nice person as well, was conveying both pleasure at seeing her and also satisfaction that she would be on top of everything for the event now that she was here and that no questions would come to him, as it should be. She gave a faint smile.

"And Remington, a pleasure. I do so enjoy when colleagues and clients are also people one genuinely enjoys. I'm certain Annelise will have already done so, but can I offer you anything?"

Rémy shot her a fleeting sideways glance, friendly, but underlaid with something else. She couldn't tell what, and it was well-hidden, but something was clearly bothering him.

"Thank you, but I'm fine. When your assistant ran into me, she offered a whole host of tantalizing options." In spite of herself, she had to admire how he'd artfully twisted the truth of her nearly plowing him down to make her sound like a great hostess. Clearly, she was dealing with a master. "I do feel bad for stopping her, though, before she even had a chance to take off her coat."

She choked on the burble of laughter that threated to escape. *Stopped me, indeed!* She must have made some sort of weird noise because both men's heads snapped toward her.

"Ah, but you are flushed, *mademoiselle*...Annelise, wasn't it?" Rémy managed to sound like he truly barely remembered her name, but his gaze, just for her, was intimate.

She nodded, not trusting herself to reply without betraying another hint of their history to her boss.

Rémy continued in a concerned tone that sounded completely natural. "We must find the cloakroom so you can get rid of your wraps." Without giving Charles a chance to say anything in response, he put one hand, so large and warm that she could feel it scorching her through all the layers she wore, on the small of her back and deftly guided her to the coatroom. Actually, he kind of pushed her. Nicely. But she didn't think she could have stopped the momentum.

"What — ?" she started to ask in a harsh whisper, but he cut her off, handing several large bills to the young coatroom attendant.

"Let us into the room and stand far enough away so that you can't hear us," he said. Amazingly, just like the young men in the ballroom had earlier, the attendant—who looked like he might be twenty at the most—nodded without even a question. He opened the door, letting them into a dark room that was lined with sumptuous red velvet and half-filled with coats. It smelled like a mix of perfume and cologne along with damp fur and fabric. The door closed, but the boy walked in front of the open window, closing the velvet curtain before he continued on his way, so that they couldn't be seen.

"Rémy," she whispered urgently, "you can't just do something like that. Someone will notice!"

He raised one dark eyebrow and took a step toward her, but she didn't back up. Her heartbeat quickened as he drew closer, his eyes intent—watching her, almost scrutinizing her. But that was crazy, wasn't it? She let out a nervous breath, feeling suddenly unsure.

"As I said earlier, the staff all know me and they know my family. I trust their discretion." He took a breath, as if he were inhaling her. He quirked his lips into a sexy, slightly crooked smile, but it was somehow sad. "And, bébé, I can read your face and body as if your feelings were written on your forehead, right there"—he tapped her forehead with one finger—"where you have a tiny little wrinkle of concentration. You wouldn't have come in here if you hadn't wanted to."

Damn it, he was totally right. She had wanted to be alone with him, and when he'd taken her by the arm, her whole body had tingled, just like it was tingling right now, blazing at his nearness, at that small, innocent touch.

Still wearing the same oddly intent expression, dark and almost...angry, he slowly undid the buttons of her coat, brushing her chest with exquisite gentleness, in contrast to the coldness she read in his eyes. She felt out of her depth, utterly. She ought to leave. This cold stranger wasn't the Rémy she'd been dreaming about for months. He wasn't even the Rémy from earlier in the day. But everything in her protested at the idea of walking away. *Not yet!* her mind screamed at her. *Just a little longer.* She didn't want this to be over. Poised on the precipice between good sense and the wild passion she felt whenever she was close to Rémy, she teetered. When he slid her coat down her arms, his warm, hard hands scorching her through her dress as he rubbed his thumbs along her sleeves, she shivered.

She sucked in a breath when he raised his arm, but he reached past her, crowding his body against hers to grab the hanger right behind her head. She smelled something spicy — soap, detergent and Rémy. She had to stop herself from licking her lips at how delicious he smelled.

When he reached around her with his other arm, basically hugging her to hang up her coat, she wanted to sway into him to close the scant couple of inches between them. Before she realized it, she was biting her lip. Rémy's eyes darkened as he looked down at her. She stepped back until she felt the cushion of coats against her spine, her chest rising and falling with her rapid breaths.

"Who told you about the cabanas? Where we met."

The question was not at all what she'd expected.

"What?" Her forehead crinkled as she thought back. "It was our office assistant. She said she'd booked a trip for someone there a few years ago who had loved the place. She's a friend. Why does that matter?"

Rémy narrowed his eyes and he didn't look like the carefree, funny man she'd met on the beach at all. He looked every inch the powerful scion of one of the wealthiest families in North America, cold and imperious.

"How can it be that we have found each other twice? It's extraordinary, my Annelise." His voice was soft, but the question was anything but gentle. His words were simple enough, but his tone was underlaid with a core of steel.

She shook her head, licking her lips in a nervous gesture she'd thought she'd grown out of. "I don't know. I was shocked when I saw you earlier, when you, um, pulled me out from under the desk."

He moved in closer so that the hardness of his body pressed against the soft front of hers. "Were you? What were you doing under there?" he asked. Softly. Dangerously.

She looked up at him with confusion and the stirrings of irritation. "Weren't *you*? Of course I was. I was plugging in some wires for the projector that they'd accidentally given to another room when... I didn't think I'd ever see you again, other than in my dreams." She shut her mouth with a snap. *Holy cow, did I actually say that out loud?*

Rémy's grim expression softened somewhat. He looked as if he were wavering, deciding. What, she really didn't know. She didn't understand where any of this was coming from. Did he think she was some kind of gold-digger? Finally, his gaze went suddenly warmer, like melted chocolate instead of glittering stones.

"I was shocked as well, that you would be here. But I have to admit I was, er...extremely pleased. It made me realize how much I'd...wished we had more time together." Something about his tone was guarded, like he wasn't saying everything, keeping her distant. A spurt of temper flared within her.

"Look, Rémy... This isn't a good idea. I don't know what's going on, but whether we both thought of each other or not, in spite of the fact that I came in here with you, I don't think this is working." She turned and started to move away, but he stayed her, circling her arm with his fingers. His grip was light, and she knew she could easily walk away...if she wanted to. But something more held her there. When she turned to him again, his face was a scant inch from her own. His eyes burned, two banked coals, smoldering in the darkness.

"Tell me you haven't thought of me in the past six months, haven't thought of me all day, and I'll step back, turn around and we can both just go back to your company's event. I'll be...charming then make some excuse in a little while." He stepped even closer, and now his body was actually brushing hers, so lightly, everywhere. She felt goosebumps rise on her arms. "But if you've thought about me even half as much as I have thought of you, come home with me tonight. Seeing you this morning, every glimpse I had of you all day...it made me remember how good we were. I wanted to get you alone. I wanted...*more*." He stood so close that they were nearly nose to nose, and his breath fanned her cheek. His slight anise smell was sweet and spicy. "Say you'll come, *bébé*, or tell me to go to hell."

He was too close, and her attraction was too powerful, for her body not to react, but the logical part of her protested. "Of course I've thought of you, Rémy. You're..." She trailed off, unable to even find the words to express all that he was, all that he meant. "You're incomparable," she finished. "Even when you're acting strange," she added. "I'll admit that you've made a convincing argument for why you're not technically a client, but you're still mostly a client at the moment, and this event is important to me and my company. There's no way I can just leave." She sighed.

When she looked at him, expecting to see distant agreement, she saw warm amusement. "Incomparable, eh?" He quirked his lips up at the corners.

She couldn't help but smile back, even as she knew it wasn't smart. "You know you are," she said in a voice grown suddenly husky.

"I've missed you," he groaned before he wrapped her tightly in his arms and slanted his mouth over hers.

His taste was just what she remembered, what she'd thought she might have idealized in her memory, but the passion and instant sizzle of attraction that flared between them was real. It was as if she couldn't get close enough as she ran her hands all over him, memorizing his broad shoulders, his muscular arms, the softness of his shaggy hair, the strength of his tight butt. He was everywhere at once, too, skimming her neck and décolletage above her dress with his lips and hands, twining his fingers into her hair and making soft pieces fall out of her updo, stroking her sides and cupping her breasts and bottom until she was gasping.

"Important, hm?" he murmured against her neck. "You're supposed to keep the clients happy at this sort of event, right?"

"Yes," she managed to gasp, even as she shivered with pleasure as he nibbled a trail of sensation down her neck and back up to her ear.

"And you consider me a temporary sort of client, right?"

He fluttered his wicked hands over her nipples, oh-so-lightly, while he brushed against her, letting her feel his hard length against her hip. Her sex clenched with need, even as her mind registered amusement at his words. He was so...exasperatingly sexy—a mix of irresistible and persistent, all wrapped up with a teasing humor. And a killer body. *Holy cow, that body. Yum.* She wanted to go with him. And...he wasn't wrong. He'd beaten her with a naughty version of her own logic.

"Say you'll come," Rémy growled against her mouth, and the vibration against the sensitive nerves of her lips sent a flood of moisture between her legs. The two of them were pressed together so tightly, their limbs intertwined, that she could feel every inch of his growing hardness against the softness of her belly. He felt amazing, then he shifted so he pressed against her sensitive pussy through their clothes, and for a second, she couldn't remember why she was resisting.

"Yes!" she said, practically panting as he continued to move, but he stilled when she put her hand on his chest. "Two conditions."

"Name them, *bébé*." He sounded wary, but she didn't miss the little growl in his voice. He wasn't unaffected by his own teasing. Far from it.

She looked into his beautiful eyes, dark with passion, and she wondered if this might be one of the most foolish things she'd ever done. Then she wondered if she really cared, since it would get her at least one more night of mind-blowing, earth-shattering pleasure with the French-Canadian sex god standing an inch in front of her. *Yep, I'm going for it.*

"One, we keep this secret. Totally secret. I don't want anyone to even suspect...well, anything."

Rémy lifted her hand and nibbled her finger. "Done. I will be totally professional whenever anyone else is present."

She shuddered as he continued on to her next fingertip, even as she forced herself to think clearly.

"Two, nothing changes after I leave. I'm going to have to work with your brother, hopefully for many years to come, and I don't want anything to be…weird. We're just two people enjoying ourselves while we're in the same place, but then you'll go back to your real life and I'll go back to mine."

She thought she saw a flash of…*something* in his eyes, but she decided she must have imagined it as a wolfish grin spread across his face — a grin of pure satisfaction.

"Agreed, *chérie*. Pure pleasure, no strings. How could I possibly refuse?" As he bent to devour her mouth again, she had the fleeting thought that she might have just made a deal with the devil himself. But she didn't care because he felt. So. Good. She could practically taste his satisfaction and passion — dark and sensual, full of need. She felt drugged with pleasure as he continued his long, searching kisses and lifted her, hiking up her skirt and nudging his thick thigh between her legs so that her aching pussy, dripping moisture, rubbed against the fabric of his pants. With every shaky breath she sucked in, she drew more of his dark spice and shameless sensuality into her.

Just when she thought that his movements would send her right over the edge, he stilled and stepped back.

She looked up at him, dazed. The mellow light of the small wall sconce was warm, glinting off of his dark hair, and his eyes were dark and fathomless in the shadows.

"Why did you stop?" she whispered.

"I wanted to look at you, wild with desire. You're so beautiful, Annelise, so sexy that you make me hurt." He rubbed the front of his pants in a blatantly sexual gesture and her belly clenched.

"Do you...want me here?" Her words were very quiet, but Rémy heard them and his eyes gleamed.

"Always, *bébé*. Anywhere. But I think we don't have time for that. Still...you're very close. People are right outside, so you'll want to be quiet." His smile was purely wicked. Before she fully realized his intent, he had knelt on the ground and pulled her full skirt over his dark head, sliding down her nylons and underwear so he could lick her.

His mouth was hot as he lapped along her seam, and she gave a little gasp but then, mindful of his warning, she tilted her head back and gave a silent scream at the pleasure. He nudged her legs wider with his fingers and the change in angle brought him even more fully in contact with the swollen flesh of her sex that was begging for his attention. The surprise and total onslaught of pleasure was too much for her, and her body crested up and over until waves of ecstasy broke over her, leaving her weak and clutching at Rémy's shoulders through her skirt. She felt lightheaded and sucked in a breath as she realized she'd been holding her breath along with the screams. Rémy gave one last lick that made her quiver then he pulled her undergarments back up and took off the boots she still wore, slipping them off gently as she leaned against the wall of the coatroom.

"You are so lovely, *bébé*." His tone was intimate, but also almost...regretful. Like some sort of apology. Then the strange moment passed. "Where are your party shoes?" he asked more prosaically.

She pointed at the large handbag she'd dropped, still not quite daring to speak.

When he pulled the velvet kitten-heeled slingbacks out of her bag, they looked ridiculously flimsy in his strong hands. He caressed the arch of each foot before he put the shoe on, and the thoughtfulness of his gesture turned something warm and gooey deep down in her chest. Some of her emotion must have shone in her expression.

"Something is wrong?" Rémy asked, watching her carefully.

She cleared her throat. "No one has ever done that...before you."

Rémy's expression was relieved for an instant then inscrutable. As if he were hiding something. "Good," was all he said, but the one word in that tone made her shiver all over again. He stood up in the ridiculously graceful way that she remembered and took her hand into his. "Let's go get through this so we can finish what we started." He leaned to whisper the words directly into her ear, and she trembled at the sensual promise in his voice. She told herself she was imagining the undercurrent of something like desperation.

She steadied herself and he took her hand in a surprisingly possessive gesture. Okay, the man was still incredible — and persuasive, even more so because she knew how amazing being with him was. She'd dreamed of little else over the past six months. He was, literally, what fantasies were made of, at least for her. But she'd worked hard for this evening too. She raised her chin. She would act like she hadn't just had an earth-shattering orgasm in the coat closet, but instead, that she'd been charming and getting to know a top client of her firm. She would meet other people. Maybe she'd even dance with Rémy. Then, at the end of the evening, she'd go home with Rémy and make wild monkey love to him all night in any position they could think of.

And after that? The logical voice at the back of her head, which she'd silenced so thoroughly earlier, was quiet but persistent. She pushed the thought away again by instead imagining what it would feel like to have Rémy on top of her again, moving within her. *And after that*, she told herself firmly, *maybe we'll do it all over again*. She refused to think beyond that.

Chapter Seven

The historical ballroom where the party was being held was just beginning to look crowded when they walked in. Right before they crossed the threshold, Rémy had brushed a warm kiss on her cheek before loosening his possessive grip and moving her so that she held his arm in a socially acceptable way. Well, socially acceptable for Montreal, anyway. Annelise had to hide a smile at the image of one of her colleagues in Boston doing the same thing. Here, though, it felt normal. And if she still felt as if every hot inch of his body was burned along her side? Well, that was her problem.

As soon as they walked in, Rémy flashed a dazzling smile at the room in general.

She leaned toward him and he bent so that his ear was close to her lips. "I'm impressed," she whispered. "If I didn't know what your real smile looked like, I would have been bowled over by this one."

Surprise then pleasure flashed behind his dark eyes, but a touch of wariness too. "I'm impressed, *petite*. And I need to work on my acting. I must be getting rusty since I've been out of the soirée game for so long." His mouth was so close to her that his soft lip brushed the top of her ear and she flushed. They were so absorbed in each other that it was a complete surprise when Annelise heard her boss's voice, close, to her left.

"There you are! I was beginning to get worried." Charles' tone was friendly, but she felt immediately guilty that he also sounded like he might have been genuinely concerned, too. He held two drinks and handed her one, her favorite for events — tonic and lime with just a splash of gin. Weirdly, Rémy tensed next to her. She didn't think Charles would notice, but it puzzled her.

Annelise opened her mouth to explain where they'd been, but Rémy beat her to it. "My apologies, the fault is all mine. I assisted Annelise with her wraps and she admired one of the paintings, so I took her to the private gallery for a quick tour. I thought she would not yet be missed, but we must have lingered too long. So many naiads and water nymphs to be seduced by," he finished smoothly, his face deliberately innocent.

Annelise almost choked on the drink she'd just sipped and managed an inelegant snort instead. Her boss looked at her in surprise. "Lots of water nymphs," she croaked, then cleared her throat. "But it was Poseidon who captivated me."

Rémy's hand gave a little squeeze on her arm, where no one would see, and her insides melted a little more.

"I've never seen the gallery," Charles replied. His face was smooth, but his tone was dubious.

Annelise was about to expand upon the beauties of the fictitious gallery — or maybe there really was one — but she was forestalled by the arrival in their little group of a striking young woman. Tall, willowy and with the waterfall of long, shiny hair that Annelise had always dreamed of, the newcomer was nothing short of dazzling. She flashed a smile, which seemed oddly familiar, and showed two rows of straight, even teeth that could have been the stars of a toothpaste commercial. Her dress was all high fashion, though — black, with crêpe and ruffles in all the right places to give the impression of casual elegance, but which probably cost a small fortune. Even her shoes were amazing, the latest season straight out of the window display of one of the high-end boutiques Annelise walked by on Newbury Street on her way to work in Boston.

When the younger woman turned her friendly gaze toward Rémy, her smile grew even wider and her eyes softened. This glamorous society beauty definitely knew Rémy well.

"Annelise, please meet my sister."

Annelise snapped away from her study of the other woman to Rémy's face. His tone was oddly gruff, significant in some way she still wasn't understanding, and she could feel his eyes burning into her.

"Clothilde, isn't it?" Annelise collected herself enough to say, extending her hand.

The young woman — now that she knew of their connection, it was obvious that the two were related — leaned forward instead of shaking her hand and kissed her on both cheeks. Annelise was a bit surprised, since she'd heard that Montrealers reserved that particular gesture more for close friends and family than the

French did, but she kissed the air on either side of Clothide's face in return. *Rémy's sister even smells expensive*, Annelise mused, but when she really looked at the younger woman, she could see the hint of great sadness that she'd once seen so often in her own eyes.

"What a pleasure to meet you. Such a pity Pierre or Luc couldn't be here," Clothilde said, and her voice held a note that Annelise didn't quite understand, almost a subtle emphasis. Rémy seemed to hear it too, she thought, as he tightened his hand again on her arm.

"You look like you've recovered. I'm so glad," Annelise said impulsively, meaning the words but realizing her mistake when her boss made a sound of surprise.

"Were you ill? Annelise, you didn't mention." Charles paused, his dark brows drawing together. "And I didn't think you'd met Pierre or Luc."

The evening was going downhill fast, and Annelise felt all of her hard work melting beneath Charles' suspicion.

"I just mentioned that Clothilde wasn't certain she'd be able to attend this evening. She had a touch of food poisoning, did you not, Clochette?" Rémy stepped in gracefully.

Clothilde went along smoothly with the lie, and her smile was utterly convincing except around her eyes. "Ah, yes, but you see now I've recovered just in time to enjoy the fun. Such impeccable organization, just as we always expect from you, Charles."

When Clothilde took Charles' arm, Annelise could have sworn that he flushed a dull red. *Incredible.* She'd never seen the suave, charming man so much as bat an eyelash, and yet it seemed even he wasn't immune to Clothilde's beauty. She led him away, asking about the latest projects, but after they'd walked a few steps, she turned and shot Rémy an unfathomable look before they continued. Rémy seemed to know what it meant, and he sighed.

When he turned back to her, though, he wore his 'social smile' again.

"Oh my, there's that smile again. Is this where I pretend to charm you, professionally, and you pretend to be charmed?" she asked, sipping her drink as she had dozens of…maybe over a hundred…times before.

Rémy's smile changed, deepening to his real smile, although something almost sad still lurked behind his eyes.

"I think we managed to allay your boss's curiosity, don't you? But it was a near thing," he commented, deftly avoiding her question. "Have you worked for him long?"

Annelise shrugged, going along with the change of subject. "Five years. And no. I think he may suspect something but…definitely not what we were actually doing."

Rémy leaned close, ostensibly to pluck a glass of champagne from the silver tray a passing waiter carried. But when his mouth was right next to her ear, he whispered, "Me kneeling under your skirt in the cloakroom, licking honey from your pussy and desperate to fuck you right there against the wall?"

Suddenly the room felt uncomfortably warm and Annelise took a shallow breath, nearly overwhelmed with the instant arousal his words brought on. He'd been right when he'd said she liked his dirty talk. Something about the way he said things just…turned her over inside and made her crazy.

"Yes," she whispered, and he brushed her arm in a way that could have been innocent, but which she was sure was deliberate, as he turned toward the stage. She realized belatedly that all the other voices had become quiet as Marie was quieting the room in preparation for Charles' speech, just as she'd asked. She saw her boss, with Clothilde still at his side, standing by the small platform. She felt a flare of pride at how well-planned the evening was proving to be, even as part of her wished she were already alone with Rémy, hearing more about what he wanted to do and telling him what she planned in return. She forced her mind back to the ballroom, and she noted with surprise that Charles had already begun to speak.

"...look forward to expanding our business partnership even more as Gaspard Industries is slated to open an additional office that will nearly double their U.S.-based interests."

A polite round of applause ensued, but, since most people didn't look shocked, Annelise assumed that it had been announced earlier. She must have missed the news while she was checking on the preparations. When she slanted a glance at Rémy from under her eyelashes, his face looked carefully blank. She'd seen that look before around countless boardrooms. Clothilde's face wore a version of the same expression, too. It was good business not to appear too pleased if things were going well—or too upset, even if they clearly weren't. It could be darn frustrating on a personal level, though.

"Now, without further ado, I want to present a plaque memorializing our thirty years of business partnership, first with Guillaume Gaspard, whom we all wish was still with us, and now with his dedicated and talented children, Pierre, Remington, Luc and Clothilde."

Rémy gave her a smile that was oddly flat as all eyes turned toward him. Then he went to the front of the room to accept the plaque jointly with Clothilde. He didn't make a formal speech, but he did say a few words, and she wasn't imagining that his glance strayed to her often.

"Thank you and *merci*, Charles. Our father always spoke highly of you and respected your work and that of your organization. I, too, appreciate the talent and intelligence of your employees, and look forward to a long and happy future."

Rémy knew that he was coming on strong, maybe too strong. And he'd lost his focus for a few minutes. But, *mon Dieu*, once he'd gotten her alone, most of his good intentions had nearly flown out of the window. Oh, he'd managed to learn a few things. He'd reeled himself in enough to feel like he could honestly gauge her reactions. He had to be careful, though. She could read him better than he'd even imagined. That thought made him feel another curious pang of something he couldn't deny was sadness. The more they talked, the more it seemed clear that she was being used, too — perhaps by her boss, Charles, or even someone else at their company. He wasn't certain and he needed to be — this was too important for even a shadow of doubt — but she just felt authentic. Her anger hadn't been an act. She'd been uneasy then annoyed, and finally, she'd been willing to walk out. Those just didn't seem like the actions of someone playing a role to get close to him.

He needed to be authentic, too. He vowed that tonight, he would try to totally let go of his suspicions and concerns, at least while he seduced her. He would say exactly what he would have said this morning or at the resort. Only afterward would he try to pump her for more information, when her defenses would be at their lowest. It wouldn't be hard to let himself just go with the moment, though, not with Annelise. She made everything sparkle.

For months, he'd thought he must have idealized her memory, that she couldn't possibly have been as vibrant and sexy, smart and witty, as he remembered. Their conversations earlier today, and their interlude in the cloakroom, had proven that, if anything, his memories couldn't even begin to compare to the real thing. He didn't know how things would play out—and he dreaded that what he would uncover would likely hurt her too—but for tonight, he'd gotten her promise that she'd come to his bed again. For now, that was enough.

It had to be.

Chapter Eight

Looking around the nearly-deserted ballroom, strewn with the usual post-party debris of empty glasses, small plates filled with half-eaten delicacies, napkins, assorted papers and even several items of clothing, Annelise felt a glow of pride. The evening had been an unqualified success. She'd spent at least an hour in intermittent conversation with Clothilde, and she'd met a number of people whose names she recognized from Charles' notes and her own research on the ownership of companies that were target prospective clients. Charles had been beaming at her when he'd said goodbye about half an hour earlier.

Even better, she'd actually really liked Clothilde. The younger woman had somber eyes, and the way she stepped once or twice had made Annelise think that she might still be recovering from her car accident, but she'd made some astute and very funny comments several times throughout their conversation. The people she'd introduced Annelise to had been some of those who were most notoriously snobbish, but they would never have dared to refuse to meet anyone with Clothilde Gaspard, a fact which wasn't lost on Annelise. She just wasn't sure what to make of it. Maybe nothing. Maybe Clothilde was just kind and polite. But Annelise wondered...and hoped? ...that maybe Rémy had said something to his sister. Which was silly, because she and Rémy were lovers and nothing more. Even so, she liked that he might have been thoughtful, even just of a lover.

Even though her feet had started throbbing in earnest — because no matter how tall or short high heels were, they inevitably started to hurt at some point or other — she made a slow tour around the gorgeous room, ensuring that everyone who was left looked like they were an employee of the hotel or the hotel's restaurant which had provided all of the food and servers. Satisfied that she could safely leave, at last, she allowed her mind to turn to Rémy.

He hadn't come to speak with her again at the party, but she'd felt his gaze, hot and intense, several times. And she'd caught herself staring at him, too, more often than she would have liked...more often than she should have. In the tux that fit him like a second skin and using expansive hand gestures as he spoke, displaying all of the innate grace she'd seen in him in Mexico, he was a sight to behold. She held the knowledge close that *that* man...that beautiful, sinfully sexy man...would be in her arms tonight, would be inside her. She shivered again in anticipation.

She'd lost sight of him when he'd walked out with Charles, but she didn't think he'd change his mind. He wasn't that kind of person. He was determined to have her, so she expected he'd come to find her. Her pulse quickened at the thought, and she felt breathless. She smiled again at the remaining crew and went back toward the lobby, stopping at the coatroom on the way to pick up her coat and the bag with her boots. It was a different attendant this time, she noted.

As she crossed to the small seating area, filled with sumptuous velvet-covered settees that looked both historically accurate and extremely inviting, she gasped when a panel in the wall opened and a strong, large hand tugged at her elbow and pulled her into a dark room. It wasn't a room, she realized as she looked around, but a hallway. She couldn't see his features clearly in the dim lights, but she thought she might recognize that tall, broad silhouette anywhere. Rémy had pulled her into a secret passage.

"Oh my gosh! What is this?" she asked, her voice breathy with the thrill and, if she were honest, the buzz of arousal she'd been feeling all evening.

"It's an old servants' passageway. Victorians and Edwardians were very status-minded, especially here where almost everyone was some sort of nouveau riche, so they liked to hide the inner workings of the household as much as possible. It's impractical in many ways, especially since they would put their kitchens so far from their dining rooms that the food would inevitably be cold by the time someone was able to walk the distance, but I've always been quite fond of the secret passages."

Annelise looked up at his face, half in shadow but still obviously animated with interest in what he was saying, and she marveled.

"I, ah...like the passage too," she said, not entirely sure how to respond to such a thorough description.

His wry laughter was loud in the narrow space. "Sorry for the mini-lecture. It's an occupational hazard. I don't think I told you that being a history professor and author is my day job. Or, at least, it has been for the last seven years or so since I mostly quit Gaspard Industries and finished my PhD in history. Nowadays I only step into the business rarely. Most of the time, anyway, although I've been doing a lot more since Clothilde's…er, for the past six months."

Annelise shook her head. "No. You're a man of untold depths," she teased.

His white smile practically glowed by the light of what she now realized were ornate golden wall sconces.

"I like your depths too," he answered suggestively, pulling her to him with one arm.

"Rémy," she breathed, looking up at his impossibly handsome face, made even more so by the mellow light. She was forcibly reminded of a picture she'd once seen of a Gilded Age tycoon in his prime — bold, confident, commanding. Even though she'd been in the same room as him for most of the evening, being this close to him again was intoxicating.

In answer, he put his other arm around her as well and kissed her, teasing her lips and tongue, and pressing against her everywhere so she was breathless and panting when he finally broke off the kiss.

"What was that for?" she whispered.

"That was for making me wait hours to hold you again, *chérie*. Torture."

Annelise laughed and stroked his cheek and the crinkles next to his eye from his smile. "Hm, but if that's my reward, you're going to make me want to torture you all the time," she teased.

"*Bébé*, you can torture me however you want. Anytime. In fact, I look forward to it," he growled, but he was interrupted by a thump from outside the door. Annelise jumped in his arms.

"Don't worry. Whoever it is won't come in," he reassured her, twining his longer fingers around hers. "Only the hotel manager and his assistant know about this passage. I keep it locked and only use it for myself."

Annelise narrowed her eyes. "Why?" she asked, her mind flashing to the hard man he'd become earlier...wondering what other secrets he kept. "If this is something that you do all the time...I'm not interested in being part of a parade." Her tone was firm.

"I use this passage to avoid being seen, yes, because I live here...on the top floor." He paused and gestured with his hand toward the length of hallway. "There's a penthouse apartment with a private elevator accessible from this passage."

She pursed her lips.

"Obviously, there have been women in my past. Several. But not nearly as many as the papers and news sites would make out. My brothers and I like to cultivate that reputation to avoid hurt feelings, since none of us are quite ready to settle down — and might never be." He stopped to take a breath and he was quiet so long that she wondered if he'd changed his mind about what he was going to say next. "For me, I think...when our mother was sick, dying actually, it was as if our father couldn't see us anymore. He died about a year after she did. People said he died of a broken heart, but I think his heart might have broken long before, when he allowed such an all-consuming passion that excluded everyone else. I believe in love, but I'm wary of it, too. I don't think it should be destructive. No child should feel that he or she is so meaningless, so unimportant."

Annelise understood that he was revealing something very important about himself. She put a tentative hand on his upper arm.

"Rémy," she said, but he shook his head, clearly not interested in saying anything else on the subject.

"I've never brought another woman I've been with through this passage or to my apartment," he finished gruffly, decisively returning to her original question.

Annelise was silent as she digested that fact. Several facts, really. The smart thing would be to keep her distance from a man who openly admitted he *wanted* to be viewed as a playboy and had no plans to settle down, who might not even be able to because of his wariness of love. Not that she wanted that anyway. Not now, not for a while. Of course, she didn't. Paradoxically, if she believed him — and she really had no reason not to — she was the first woman to kiss him here in this secret passageway. She'd be the first to make love with him where he lived. She honestly didn't know how she felt about that. Or, rather, she knew she liked it, but also that she shouldn't. *But, well, I do.*

She took his hand again, reveling in the contrast of his rough palm and fingers against her softer skin. "Lead the way, then, Professor."

He quirked up his lips as he inclined his head, and he led her down the rest of the narrow passage. It opened onto a very small vestibule room, which had another door leading to it as well. The outside doors to the elevator were plain, but when the elevator arrived, there was an inner set as well that were dazzlingly shiny gold, with lions and suns carved in deep relief.

"Wow!" she couldn't help but exclaim. "I think these put the 'gilded' in 'Gilded Age', she quipped, and Rémy chuckled.

"I guess they *are* a little ostentatious," he agreed.

"A little? I think I just got a sunburn." The sound of his deep chuckle echoed into the elevator as they stepped onto it. She had to do a full spin, slowly, to look at all of the details.

"This is gorgeous — and beautifully restored. I've seen a lot of Victorian and Edwardian buildings. Heck, I even hosted a party for my company in one of the Newport mansions in Rhode Island. I think this is better than any of them. The ballroom is fantastic, and this elevator? Wow. Who did the restoration?" She trailed her finger along the curlicue design between two of the mirrors.

Rémy coughed. "I did," he admitted. "Well, obviously I worked with a number of craftsmen as well, but I oversaw the work everywhere in the hotel. I've done a few projects like this for some of the properties my family owns."

She spun around to look at him again, seeing him in an entirely new light. Clearly his passion for history extended to architecture and art. What he'd done was stunning.

As the elevator moved, she realized he'd pressed the top button, which had a surprisingly modern code machine next to it so that Rémy could key in some sort of passcode. She marveled at how expensive something like that must be in a luxurious, historical building right downtown. Montreal was less expensive, sure, but in Boston, it would have been millions. The tiny one-bedroom apartment in Boston that she'd thought was so cozy suddenly seemed very far away.

"I'm impressed…deeply impressed, which is saying a lot because I've been falling in love with all of the architecture in the city. And the people! Everyone has been so warm and friendly."

"I'm sure they *have* been nice to you," Rémy grumbled. "A beautiful, intelligent, charming girl…alone."

Annelise glanced at him in real surprise. He sounded…jealous? Definitely possessive. She tapped his forearm, and he caught her hand and held it.

"Not *that* friendly," she said. "Get your mind out of the gutter, Monsieur Gaspard."

"My mind never leaves the gutter when you're nearby," he answered with an exaggerated leer that made her laugh again. But when he pulled her closer, his face was intent. "You make me wild, *chérie*. You. Your face, your skin, your scent, your voice. I can't get enough."

Annelise felt a warmth spreading throughout her body that was a mixture of sensual anticipation and…something else, something deeper and more affectionate, something she didn't want to examine too closely if she was going to be able to leave. She was saved from answering by the melodic bell of the old-fashioned elevator as it arrived at the penthouse.

Her sharp breath of appreciation was loud in the marble-floored, mirrored hallway.

"You like it?" Rémy asked, his hand warm and solid again on the small of her back.

"It's beautiful, like stepping back in time to Montreal's most glamorous era. It's so spacious, too. Right in the heart of downtown."

Rémy seemed pleased by her comments. "It was a lot more modern when we bought the hotel, a sleek place for the former owner to stay temporarily. When I decided to live here, I wanted to both update everything that was getting worn out and also to bring back the character as much as possible. The decorator I worked with even managed to find a group of pieces that were going to be thrown away after a museum rejected them as a donation, so we sent them to be restored as well."

The level of wealth that Rémy must possess, to be able to just casually redecorate and restore a prime penthouse, including museum-quality furniture? It blew her mind.

"Well, you did an awesome job," she said, stroking the smooth satinwood carved arm of one chair in the entryway. She could see into the living room as well as the dining room. Everything was all spacious-feeling, with a semi-open floor plan, but somehow the touches and architecture managed to keep it authentic and historical as well.

Rémy shrugged, but he couldn't quite hide the pride from his expression. Then his eyes took on a mischievous glint. He took her coat and other wraps from her for the second time that evening, tucking her gloves into her pocket and her scarf into one sleeve, like the true cold-weather dweller that he was.

"Let me put your coat in the closet and I'll show you the bathroom. Parts of it aren't authentic, but I think you may still like it."

Annelise felt a smile tug at the corners of her mouth. Whatever was in the bathroom, it wasn't just period-era fixtures. But she'd play. With Rémy, it seemed she was always game.

When he led her down the hall to a plain white door, she wasn't sure what to expect, but whatever she'd imagined, the enormous room that lay behind, totally surrounded by windows overlooking the lights of the Montreal skyline, was beyond her imagining. She laughed when she saw that, indeed, there was a beautifully preserved clawfoot tub with gold fixtures. She'd bet it was probably real gold, too. Even the old-fashioned toilet had a pull-chain with a gold knob sculpted like a lion.

"Fabulous," she breathed, tracing the eyes of the knob. When she turned around, she saw Rémy, and what he stood next to made her eyes go wide with surprise. Somehow, the man had a giant-sized hot tub right there, surrounded by historical black-and-white tile.

"Oh my goodness! Holy cow! I would have to swim to cross that thing!" she exclaimed, walking toward it to put her fingers into the hot water. It was invitingly steamy, and the water was just the right sort of hot when she stuck her hand in.

She turned back to Rémy, shaking her head incredulously. "I can't believe you have the mother of all hot tubs in your historical penthouse hotel suite!"

Rémy had come closer, so he stood nearer to her than she'd realized, close enough to touch her...or push her into his mini-pool. She nearly giggled at the image. He shrugged again and pursed his lips in the way she'd come to recognize as being almost as common in Montreal as it was in other French-speaking countries.

"I love history—don't get me wrong—but I do love some modern comforts too much to give them up."

"Of course," she teased. "Going without a hot tub is practically the same as going without indoor plumbing."

"You mock me, *chérie*?" He raised one dark eyebrow in a gesture that made her heart quicken.

"They didn't have professors like you when I was in college. We had one youngish English professor who always managed to untuck one side of his shirt and we thought he was positively debonair. You must have a line of female students waiting to get into your office hours." She was saying the first thing that popped into her head to distract him, but Rémy was undeterred as he took a step closer. She would have backed up, but there was nowhere to go except into the steaming water.

Rémy shook his head slowly. "No-o, at least, not anymore. I haven't taught for a couple of years — only lectured. Although, I suppose I did have some over-eager female students in the past. I would have liked to have had you in my classes, though, *bébé*. With that sharp mind of yours…and sharper tongue."

"What would you have said to me during your office hours?" she asked, more breathless than she realized. The warmth from the hot tub had made her cheeks flush and one strand of hair stuck to her face, reminding her of when they'd been alone together in the Caribbean.

Rémy stepped very close, so that he was crowding her, and his chest just brushed her breasts when she took a breath. He quirked up one side of his mouth and she could tell he was amused, enjoying their conversation.

"Well, first I would have put up a sign telling all the other students that office hours were canceled."

Annelise's burst of laughter was loud in the quiet room. She poked his nose. "That's not very professional."

"Ah, but you asked if *you* had come. You can't possibly expect me to remain professional with a goddess in my office." Rémy waggled his eyebrows. "Now, where was I? Oh, yes, we were totally alone, you in a plaid skirt and sweater…"

She laughed again. "I never wore that in college!"

Rémy looked her up and down suggestively. "Then you should have."

"I don't think so," she answered, trying to sound quelling but unable to keep the smile off her face.

"But of course, *chérie*. You would be wearing a trench-coat, which you would take off as soon as I locked the door."

"What?" she said in an outraged tone. "Like a flasher?"

Rémy swayed toward her so his front pressed against her, and so that she could smell his spicy, warm scent. "Exactly like that," he growled.

"You have quite the imagination, Professor Gaspard," she scolded, but the effect was ruined by her sigh of pleasure as he stroked one hardened fingertip down her cheek.

"Don't make me imagine, then, my Annelise. I've been picturing you without this dress on all night. It's been so long, *bébé*." His voice was strangled and gravelly at once.

Annelise looked away. "I'm sure there were other naked women to remind you of what we look like."

Rémy tipped her chin up with his fingertip so she had to look at him. His eyes intent on hers, he shook his head. "No. There have been no others since we parted."

His words made her shiver with longing, and her core went damp. She didn't know if she believed him but, oh, she wanted to. She swayed toward him and he caught her in his arms as if he'd been expecting her. She fit perfectly. She could smell a hint of chlorine from the water, a faint whiff of his cologne, but mostly he just smelled warm, almost like home.

It seemed like the most natural thing in the world when he turned her around slowly to unzip her dress. He pressed kisses on the skin down her spine as he uncovered her back, inch by inch, so that when he let her dress fall to her waist, she shuddered with pleasure. Next, he unclipped her bra, and as it loosened, he replaced it with his hands, kneading and caressing her breasts as he kissed her neck and ear from behind. When she would have turned around, he stopped her.

"Ah, *non*, *chérie*. I want you to be totally naked when you turn around. I've dreamed of this. Would you deny a man so long starved for your beauty?"

Even as his hands were magical on her nipples, rolling them between his fingers until she thought she was losing her mind, she had to smile at the outrageousness of his statement. "Starved for my beauty?" she laughed, ending on a gasp as he bit her lightly, making her nerves go extra sensitive.

"Yes, don't I seem hungry?" he answered, and his voice did have an edge.

She moaned and he pulled the rest of her dress down, taking her panties and pantyhose down with it. She stepped out of her heels just in time to avoid falling over as he knelt behind her. He slid against her all the way down, and the sensation of the fabric of his tuxedo against her bare skin was delicious. Sensual. When he lifted each foot up to take her legs out of her hose, she leaned against the side of the hot tub, feeling the steam rise so that her skin was moist and warm. He nipped one of her buttocks, which was right in front of his face, and she yelped, turning her head.

His expression was somehow both sensual and sheepish, with his dark hair mussed. "I had to. They look like peaches…round and ripe, and they were right in front of me. It would take a saint to resist your spectacular ass. And, *bébé*, I'm *not* a saint."

"Well then, you'd better keep going, because the other side is jealous," she said, and was satisfied to see the surprise and wonder that crossed his face.

"*Oh la*, you were made for me, weren't you?" he murmured, and kissed her other butt cheek, ending with a hard nip. This time, the sensation made her channel clench with need, and she felt suddenly empty.

"Can I turn around now?" she asked.

"Please," he groaned, still kneeling. His voice was strangled, and his face was lit a wild, almost Caribbean blue by the light from inside the hot tub.

As she turned, she gave an extra wiggle and shake, and loved seeing how it made his eyes follow her slightest motion. He looked as if he were memorizing her, enrapt with the sight of her body. *Her*, Annelise. It was still a bit incredible. She often felt…ordinary, but he looked at her as if she was something extraordinary. And then, somehow, it felt as if she were extraordinary.

"My goddess has returned," he said, half-teasing and half-reverent.

"Aren't you going to pay tribute to me, then?" she answered imperiously, but she couldn't stop her mouth from curving upward.

"I'm already on my knees, *chérie*," he reminded her, "for the second time this evening." He looked thoughtful. "There is one thing missing, though, for my perfect fantasy." Before she realized what he was going to do, he had picked her up and she was falling right into the warm water of the mega-tub.

When she surfaced, she looked at him indignantly.

"You weren't wet, *bébé*. Sea goddesses should always be wet," he teased.

She stood, and the feeling of all of the water running down her as he watched every drop, tracing their movements with his eyes, was glorious. He looked happy and…hungry. That was it. He looked ravenous. She couldn't be too mad.

"You didn't check," she said in a throaty voice that she barely recognized. "I was definitely already wet." She did a slinky, slow walk across to the other side of the hot tub, and she could feel his eyes practically burning her as she went. When she turned and sat down on the opposite edge, every line of his body was tense.

She held his gaze with hers and spread her legs, showing him the moisture trickling from her pussy, showing him what he did to her.

"I think it's time for my show now," she said, still amazed at her own boldness but growing more comfortable. Rémy brought out a sensual, sexual side to her that she hadn't really explored before.

She'd never seen a man get undressed so fast as Rémy, taking his tux jacket and shirt off. She was pretty sure that she heard a couple of buttons—or maybe cufflinks?—tinkle as they hit the tile floor.

Rémy continued to hold her gaze as he moved, mesmerizing her. He looked fierce and powerful, and as he uncovered a chest that was even more muscular than she remembered, he looked almost savage.

"Touch yourself, *chérie*. I have longed to see that."

The sensual command in his deep voice made her give an inward shudder as her innermost muscles clenched. She had to obey. More, she wanted to.

She reached down, tentatively at first. Then, encouraged by the way his eyes heated and his mouth tightened as he followed her movements, she began stroking her own sex, slick from the moisture of her arousal. As she brushed her fingertips up and down her slit, swirling it around her sensitive clit, she gasped but she didn't let her head fall back. She loved watching Rémy's face too much.

"Is that how you touched yourself when we were apart?" He lightly rubbed the growing bulge at the front of his pants as he prompted her. "Did you think of me?"

His words evoked memories of how she'd lain in bed with her eyes closed, imagining it was his hands touching her again. She nodded her acknowledgment, not entirely comfortable but still unashamed by the admission.

"Ah, *bébé*, you don't know how much I love that you did that," he growled and rubbed the growing bulge at the front of his pants.

"Then you'd better come and show me," Annelise challenged, feeling reckless with arousal — and powerful, seeing how she affected him.

Rémy's eyes blazed like chocolate fire and he unfastened his trousers, letting his long, thick cock spring free. He let the rest of his clothes just crumple to the ground, next to hers, before he jumped into the hot tub in one fluid leap and sloshed across to her, uncaring of the water splashing.

When he would have knelt again, she shook her head and instead motioned him closer with her finger.

"No…I think I need to do some worshiping of my own, Rémy," she murmured, transfixed by how hard and swollen he'd grown. It was a good thing it had been dark in Mexico or she might have been concerned about how he'd fit inside her. Now, though, all she wanted was to touch him.

He looked like he might refuse, but something in her face must have stopped him because he stepped closer to her, his face taut with desire. A muscle in his jaw twitched as she watched him, and she felt more moisture gush to her core as the wiry hair on his legs brushed her open thighs. His cock was in the perfect position for her appreciation, in the form of licking and sucking.

She kissed the tip slowly at first. She hadn't done this often with her ex-fiancé because he hadn't been comfortable with it, but she'd always wanted to. She'd barely started to do this with Rémy in Mexico — and she froze when he moaned as if it were torn from him.

"Good or not good?" she asked, wanting to learn, wanting to give this to him.

Rémy looked down at her in surprise. After a quick study of her face, he cupped her cheek with one large hand. "Very good, Annelise. Beyond good. You can do anything you want to any part of me, especially that part." His voice was like rich velvet, smoothing over her nerves. "You do everything right. I've never felt anything like your hot little mouth on me."

Her nipples hardened to tight little points at his words and the sincerity behind them. All of the desire that had been muted momentarily came back in a rush, even more intensely. She leaned again to take him into her mouth, savoring the salty-spicy taste of him. Now that she knew he was enjoying everything, she relished the noises he made as she swirled her tongue around him, sucking, licking and using her hands to stroke him as well. After a few minutes, he tugged gently at her hair, making her scalp tingle deliciously, until she released him with a pop and looked up at him.

"I'm sorry, *bébé*, because I wanted to give you as long as you wished, but if I don't stop you now, I'll explode in your mouth. I hope you're ready, because I need to be inside you. *Now*." The last word was almost a grunt, it was so guttural, and his face was a mask of need.

Annelise shivered and opened her thighs in blatant invitation. "I think I might always be ready for you, Rémy," she admitted. He reached down to feel her wetness, and his smile was dark and full of promise.

"Good," was all he said before he pulled her into the water and knelt so he could plunge into her so deeply that it made her tremble. She felt full and stretched in a way she never had been, and it was incredible.

"So. Sexy," he ground out as he started to move in deep, rhythmic thrusts. The hot water lapped at her nipples, which were tight from the cooler air as her breasts bobbed on the surface. It added another layer of unexpected pleasure. He braced himself with his arms on the edge of the tub, one on either side of her head, and she turned to kiss one of his hard forearms. He bent down and pulled one of her nipples into his mouth and it made pleasure rise and spiral rapidly throughout her body until it burned almost out of control.

She strained up to meet him, reveling in the sensation of being taken. Totally joined, absolutely in synch. When she managed to open her eyes to look at him, his expression was taut. Intense. His eyes were dark and fathomless, and something in them made her nearly topple over the edge of pleasure.

She could feel the waves he made from his thrusting all around them, and she heard water splashing onto the floor, but Rémy didn't slow. In fact, he sped up until he was pistoning into and out of her at a furious pace. When he reached down to grab her hips, holding her up in a way that seemed almost super-human, he plunged his cock in even more deeply and it touched something inside her that sent her headlong into a wave of pure bliss, sailing over the edge of pleasure into nirvana. She only vaguely heard his hoarse yell as he thrust into her one last time, then she felt a hot flood as he released his seed. He shuddered and his shoulders shook with the force of his pleasure, and while she felt limp and totally relaxed, she still shook periodically, as well, from the after-quakes of such a strong release.

He tenderly cradled her head and let himself sort of fall backward and to the nearest seat along the edge of the pool where he collapsed with her on top of him. He settled her so that she lay straddling him with his still-hard cock remaining pressed deeply into her, and he nestled her head into the crook between his neck and shoulder.

They lay there like that for a long time—she wasn't sure how long—until she finally felt like she'd regained the power of movement in her arms and legs.

"Oh my God," she groaned.

"You still think I'm a deity, either because I have a magical cock or because I have accidentally hypnotized you. Frankly, I don't care which it is." She could hear the smile in his voice, although she couldn't see his face.

She managed a watery laugh before she tilted her head so she could see the right side of his face, including his right eye. Moving her head more seemed unthinkable at the moment, so she contented herself with the half-view of his self-satisfied smile.

"You know, I should, but I don't care either." She snorted. "Magical cock!"

She felt Rémy's chuckle rumbling in his chest more than she heard it.

"Enchanted dick?" He flexed his hips, eliciting a gasp from her as his semi-hardness rubbed against the sensitive sides of her inner walls.

"Ah-mmmmm," she moaned, and Rémy flexed again. She could feel him growing larger again, stretching the sensitized walls of her channel.

"I'm going to take that as your agreement, *chérie*." His eye crinkled at the corner, and she thought that he must smile a lot to have those exact smile lines. "I'd like to take you all over again, but I think I'd better give you a break. I don't want you to be sore."

She might have worried it was just some sort of line, but she heard real regret in his voice. She shivered as he reluctantly slid out of her, rubbing along every sensitized nerve. Then he lifted her into his arms, cradling her against his chest as he rose like some sort of sea god out of the water.

"We've been in here too long already, *bébé*. Let's go try somewhere new for us, like the bed."

"I'm too heavy!" she protested. "You can't carry me."

Rémy's mouth made that Gallic moue that she was beginning to be addicted to. "Watch me." And he put action to words, carrying her to the bed where he deposited her, still dripping. Almost before she'd finished laughing, Rémy was already returning with several large towels. Her mouth went dry at the sight of him, stark naked, his darker brown skin set off by the crisp white of the towels. She had the errant thought that he should be naked all the time.

Her smile faded when she surprised a fleeting look on his face. He didn't look happy and teasing — or nearly as relaxed as she'd thought he should be. Instead, he looked grim. But it was only there for an instant, so she guessed it must have been a trick of the light. Or maybe she just told herself that, not wanting to dim the pleasure of the evening. She firmly put the strange moment out of her mind.

Chapter Nine

Rémy wasn't certain who enjoyed his slow, thorough drying of Annelise with his fluffy towels more, her or him. Probably him, but only because it allowed him to see every gorgeous, naked inch of her wet body again and to touch her everywhere. Still, while Annelise was still gloriously sensitive and responsive, he couldn't ignore the sinking feeling in the pit of his stomach. The growing dread and distaste for what he was about do was even more of an insult now that they'd had incredible sex with such magnificent abandon. In a different time, he thought, he really could have grown to love her, might already be growing to, now. He pushed the thought away determinedly and refocused himself on what he had to do.

He dried himself quickly and slid into the bed with her, settling himself so that she nestled right next to him with her head on his right shoulder, and he turned to curve his leg over hers, entwining them. With his free arm, he pulled the bedcovers up over them, and then settled in with a sigh of contentment, kissing the hair at her temple.

"Okay, now I can never look at a hot tub the same way again. Ever. The clawfoot tub in my new apartment that I was so proud of is going to look awfully small, too." She gave a silvery laugh and he felt the vibrations against his chest.

It was the perfect opening. He took a deep breath. "And what is your life like in Boston, then, hm? What do you do when you're not running large events or seducing hapless travelers with your luminous beauty, I wonder?"

She lifted her head to look at him, and her smile cut him to the core. He wished he could always have that look in his mind, to call up the memory. She was still flushed and sated from their lovemaking, pleased by his wanting to know more.

"Well, I've been spending a lot of time with my friends, visiting places I always wanted to but never seemed to be able to convince my ex-fiancé to go — a whale watch on Cape Cod, a cider-tasting in Vermont. I visited a couple of the historical house museums... I think you'd like those, Professor."

"Oh, *absolument*. I'm certain I would. And your office is in a historic part of the city too, isn't it?"

"You did your homework, huh? Or did your brother tell you? He's been to a few meetings with Charles in Boston in the last few months. Yeah, we're in the Copley area, just a couple blocks from Newbury Street, close to the Common and the Public Garden. It's a great location."

Rémy covered his surprise. Pierre hadn't mentioned that he'd met with Charles Pinkston in Boston. Normally, when Rémy was working as a professor, that wouldn't have been odd. But these past few months, he'd been almost as involved in the family business as he'd been right after their parents had died. Rémy had known his brother had been to Boston a couple of times, arranging things for their new U.S. headquarters, but…he really didn't know what to make of the supposed meetings. He would double-check with Pierre but he was nearly certain that whoever had met with Charles Pinkston hadn't been his brother. That made them a distinct inconsistency, and with at least two attacks on his family, he needed to carefully consider anything unusual.

"You seem like you enjoy your work very much. Should I be jealous of Charles?"

Her eyes were surprised, then amused. "Um, Charles is a great mentor. I mean, you've met him. He's a great combination of suave and knowledgeable, really smart and motivated, but he keeps a pretty decent balance between work and home. Or, he did. His wife passed away a couple of years ago, and his daughter is in college. Now I think he might work a little too much. I try to take care of him a bit…make thing easier. It's my job, but also something I enjoy, especially for someone I respect and admire as well. That's as far as my feelings for him go, though."

The picture she was painting of her boss was tame enough, and yet, there was something he couldn't put his finger on. Something was niggling at the back of his mind.

"Still, a wealthy, handsome widower? And he seems to find you indispensable."

She turned and pulled a face. "I like him, personally *and* professionally. But he treats me more like a daughter than anything else, constantly telling me to take good care of myself and trust my instincts, and I respect him. Why all the questions about Charles?"

"I guess I don't understand how someone could work with you every day and not want to make love to you." Rémy knew he had to back off, so he switched gears. "Your eyes don't seem as sad now," he remarked. That was the first thing he'd noticed after he'd gotten over the shock of seeing her again, here, in Montreal. Her beautiful sea-blue eyes were no longer heavy with sorrow and grief. "I'm glad."

Annelise nodded. "No. Our time in Mexico? It really helped me to get beyond my grief and put an end to that chapter." She smiled a little as she looked up at him. "Oh, I still think about Kyle from time to time. He was my closest friend and lover for many years, after all, but I can say his name without aching, and when I see something that reminds me of him, I don't start to cry. You—us being together—it reminded me of all of the wonderful, unexpected possibilities that are still out there to be discovered. My relationship ended, and it broke my heart and my trust, but I won't let it—or him—break my spirit. There's so much beauty in this world."

Rémy forced a smile, but he felt like she'd shot him through the heart. "And I brought you to that realization? I must be even better-looking than I realized." He thought he sounded light and charming, but he must have betrayed some of his underlying emotions.

"What's bothering you, Rémy? Earlier, you were acting so strangely. And now...you're saying one thing, but your eyes are saying something else entirely." She moved back, subtly but unmistakably, so their bodies weren't touching as they had been.

He sighed, torn between wanting to believe his instincts about her innocence and protecting his family. He settled on a half-truth somewhere in between.

"I'm on edge. The accident was as bad as everyone feared. There was a malfunction in Clothilde's car when she was driving, alone, near our house. The only lucky thing is that she realized it and was able to slow slightly before her car skidded in the rain. She could have gone right over the riverbank into the Saint-Laurent, but instead, she was caught by a tree along the road. When I arrived, she was in intensive care and her life hung in the balance." As the horror of the memories washed over him, he reminded himself that she was all right. Still, the image of her, so pale, looking as though she might already be dead in that hospital bed, would haunt him forever.

His voice cracked on his next words. "We...worried that she might not fight to come back. She had been so sad and" —he made a gesture of helplessness—"for a short while, very short, we worried it might have been something she'd done on purpose, but we knew...*we knew* she would not do such a thing. In fact, someone had tampered with her car."

"Oh my God! Did they catch the person?" Annelise's concern was palpable—and her shock.

"No." Rémy shook his head. "And it has been something that has consumed us all as she has recovered. Our wealth has put us at greater risk in the past, particularly of kidnapping. That's something we grew up with, prepared for, but this—an attack to harm—was beyond what we would ever have expected. We have hired several private detectives. None of us will rest until the *bâtard* is brought to justice." He released her hand when he realized he was squeezing it too hard. Even as the familiar rage rose inside him, he forced himself to stay calm, to watch her reactions. The horror on Annelise's face seemed genuine. *Can she be that good an actress?*

"God, Rémy, how awful. I'm so sorry that happened to her...to your family." The words were simple but heartfelt. His smile in return was tight. Damn it. He *hated* doing this.

"The only good thing to come out of this — and I can hardly believe I am saying this — is that nearly dying seems to have brought Clothilde back to life. She hasn't spoken of it, but...I think it scared her. She has worked tirelessly to regain her health and strength."

"Yes, she looked amazing at tonight's party," Annelise interjected, but she couldn't entirely stifle the yawn she tried to hide. Rémy realized it must be getting incredibly late.

He nodded. "Thank you, *petite*. She fought through the therapy and now she only has a few scars. She still tires more easily, but otherwise" — his voice cracked again — "it could have been so much worse. Instead, we have our sister back." He grimaced, but in a good-natured way. "Correction... Our sister with even more attitude. But she could be ten times...no, fifty times bossier...and I would still love her."

"Fifty times!" Annelise laughed.

"Okay, you're right. That isn't humanly possible, considering her current level of bossiness, but...you get the picture." Rémy chuckled and Annelise laughed again, but it ended on another stifled yawn. Rémy gathered her even closer, wanting to touch her everywhere but knowing they both needed to rest.

"*Bébé*, I wanted to make love to you all night long, but it's late. Shall we sleep then make wild love again in the morning?"

"Mmm, I want to argue, but I'm so comfortable. Wild love...definitely."

Rémy chuckled at her half-asleep tone. She was clearly already drifting off, and he knew he'd follow her soon after. "Goodnight, my Annelise," he whispered.

His last thought before succumbing to the embrace of sleep himself was that, if only things had been different, he might have gotten to hold her like this every night. He was asleep before he could examine how many different ways that was wrong.

Chapter Ten

When Annelise finally cracked her eyes open, she immediately squinted against the light. Based on the length of the shadows filtering into the bedroom, it was already well into the morning. Thank goodness she'd scheduled today as a free day, so no one should be looking for her right away this morning. She stretched, feeling delicious aches and soreness in muscles she wasn't sure she'd ever felt before. A smile danced on her lips. Rémy had woken her up twice more during the night to make love again. He'd said he couldn't wait. The man was insatiable and...creative. He'd seemed nearly desperate to have her, as if each time might be the last time.

The recollection brought her up short. He was gone, it seemed. She looked around the room, and while everything was rumpled, just as they'd left it, she didn't hear him in the bathroom or the kitchen. She swung her legs over the side of the bed, and her eyes lit on what looked like a soft T-shirt of his. She grabbed it and pulled it on, chuckling when it reached to around mid-thigh when she stood up. She felt better covered — or sort of covered, anyway — as she went in search of him. He could be any number of places, she reasoned. It wasn't exactly like she'd gotten a full tour last night in their beeline to the bathroom and hot tub. Her cheeks flushed all over again as she recalled their time there. She had been so free and uninhibited — and she didn't regret one second.

What Rémy had revealed about himself and the real fear his family had felt after Clothilde's attack and during her recovery had genuinely surprised her. She'd been so wrong when she'd instantly assumed that he was nothing more than a rich playboy, as soon as she'd found out who he was. It seemed that all of their enormous wealth and privilege hadn't protected Clothilde, not from her earlier heartbreak and not from her accident. In fact, it had probably made her more of a target. Annelise wished she could comfort him, do something to help. *But he didn't ask for my assistance*, a little voice reminded her. She ignored the voice, but she still felt a little...hesitant. She supposed it was only natural after the way her trust had been so broken by Kyle. She was definitely recovering, but she didn't know if her heart would ever be the same. In fact, she was sure that it wouldn't. It would always be something pieced back together, but often scars healed stronger than the original skin. She wouldn't ever blindly fall madly in love with someone, giving all of her heart, love and trust in one fell swoop. It wasn't that she wouldn't love...just that it could never be the way it had been. She just wasn't that young or naïve anymore.

She gave a wry laugh as she realized the direction of her thoughts. As she was telling herself how she wouldn't blindly love and trust again, she knew that she was already starting to care for Rémy. There. She'd admitted it to herself. In spite of all her better judgment, without fully and logically evaluating everything and without even knowing countless things about him, she could feel her affection growing. The part of her that was still wounded, that made the doubting voice rise within her... That part wouldn't let her admit that it might be anything more, because then she might get hurt again. And for Rémy to hurt her, after all of the beautiful moments they'd shared, might just break her in a way that Kyle's betrayal hadn't.

As she padded through the condo, she glanced appreciatively at the beautiful period décor again, even lovelier in the daylight than it had been at night, and found her way to the kitchen. It was a chef's dream, with copper pots and pans hanging everywhere and rows of beautifully etched glass stemware displayed in glass cases. She saw a note scrawled in a man's hand in the middle of the counter. The signature confirmed it must be Rémy's. Strange that she'd never seen his handwriting but she liked it — bold, but beautiful, like the man himself. His note was short but thoughtful.

Good morning, chérie.
Had to run downstairs for some urgent business. You looked so lovely, didn't want to wake you. Back ASAP.
Bisous,
R

She smiled and her stomach rumbled. A quick look in the fridge revealed a couple of takeout containers, milk and a block of cheese of questionable age. She groaned, but she wasn't surprised. She frequently didn't have time to make it to the grocery store herself when she was busy at work, and the sub shop down the street knew her by name when she called at least once a week. But she needed energy if they were going to do anything more like they had done the night before. Her heart sped at the thought. Rémy was...amazing — funny, handsome, smart and like a dream lover. She could hardly believe they'd had the chance to be together again. If she believed him, he'd been thinking about their time in Mexico for six months, too.

With a possible lazy morning — or maybe even day in bed in mind — she decided she'd run out and look for a bakery. She thought she'd seen a few signs that said *Boulangerie*, or, failing that, she was pretty sure she'd seen a Tim Hortons a couple of blocks away. The chain of coffee shops seemed to be everywhere when she traveled to Canada — like Dunkin' Donuts in Boston — but she secretly preferred the coffee at Tim Hortons, although she could never admit it to her New Englander friends. Her stomach growled again, and she spun around. When her eyes landed on her coat and shoes in the half-open closet near the front door, she realized she didn't really have to put anything else on. Sure, it would be a little wicked, but she'd be totally covered by her long coat. And she might beat Rémy back to his suite, anyway. If she did get back after him, she could surprise him with food and with herself, giftwrapped in only a T-shirt and coat.

She hummed happily as she got ready, grabbing her purse from where she'd dropped it in the entryway, and setting out. It was strangely erotic, being practically naked under her heavy coat, made even more so because no one in the hotel lobby would know. She imagined what Rémy's face would look like if she pulled her coat up slowly, just enough so he'd know she wasn't wearing anything on her bottom half. Where before she'd hoped to beat him back to his place, now she hoped she'd run into him. Then, a more prosaic thought popped into her head. She had already come down in the elevator but didn't know the passcode to enter into the keypad to get back up.

As if he'd been conjured by her wishes, just as she was slipping out of the secret door, she saw him from across the lobby, stepping into one of the numerous alcoves off the larger space. She thought it had something to do with the period in which the hotel had been built, but there were countless little spaces and multiple landings for staircases. She'd noticed in passing that most of them seemed to be set up as small sitting areas. Thrilled with her stroke of good luck in spotting him, she hurried across the hotel lobby to follow him. He was sitting, looking at something on his phone, as she approached. When she was only a couple of feet away, she realized he was actually talking on his phone as well. She froze at what he said.

"I didn't get as much from her as I'd hoped, but I think it's enough to go on."

Confusion, denial, then a sick sort of dread washed over her in quick succession. Who was he talking about? But she suspected she already knew.

He still hadn't seen her, inadvertently half-hidden as she was by a wing-back chair upholstered in a pastel dusky-rose velvet. She felt rooted to the spot as he waited, listening to whoever was on the other end of the line.

"Yes, I definitely think an even deeper check on the boss, financials, family, everything you can find. Circumstances of his wife's recent death, info about any trouble his college-age daughter might be in. And" — he sighed, rubbing the back of his neck — "you'd better run another one on A too, even more comprehensive than before — current debts, account balances, known associates, the whole works. I'm pretty sure now that she's clear, especially since Marie verified her story, but we need to be a hundred percent certain. And run basic searches on all the employees of the company, just to see if anyone else throws up a red flag. Start with the receptionist. I don't know her name, but she could be somehow involved."

All of the happiness and optimism, the extra bounce she'd been feeling since she'd opened her eyes — no, since she'd seen Rémy again — disappeared, just drained right out of her there onto the gleaming marble floor, leaving her feeling cold and unutterably sad. He'd been using her. While she'd been giving herself to him, enjoying every touch, every smile, everything, he'd been somewhere else. It occurred to her that she didn't even know who he was.

Part of her wanted to turn around, walk away and never look back. But a larger part of her, the part that she'd only begun to understand when she'd walked through the fire of betrayal before, sparked to life again. She was devastated, yes, but she was also furious. *How dare he? Who the hell does he think he is that he can treat people like that? Treat* me *like that?*

Without conscious thought, her feet carried her the last few feet until she was standing next to him, glaring until he looked up. She realized that, if she hadn't happened to see him step over here, it would have been a great place for a private conversation. She never would have known.

The expression on his face was surprised but also oddly resigned, almost as if he'd been waiting for this, expecting it. He didn't look guilty, though, or even remotely contrite. Or maybe her rage was just too great for her to see anything but what an ass he apparently was.

"Gotta go. Talk later. Bye." He clicked to disconnect his call, despite the man's voice still talking on the other end.

"You were talking about me, I assume." It wasn't a question, but Rémy gave a curt nod.

"There are certain facts that connect someone in your company to a break-in at my house, as well as possibly to the attack on my sister and to an attack on one of my brothers. What we've found out so far points strongly to your boss, Charles." He looked grim and his mouth was tight. "I have to find out whatever I can, to protect my family."

Every word felt harsh, like further confirmation of how little she meant to him. A distant, logical part of her could almost understand his reasoning, but not how he'd chosen to handle things with her. She stared down her nose at him, keeping her spine straight and her shoulders back.

"I'm sorry for what happened to your family. I'm sorry that being a target of attacks has made you so cynical..." She sucked in a harsh breath as her voice cracked before she continued. "But it does not give you the right to treat someone this way, to act the way you did with me." She hated that her eyes were starting to burn, but she refused to let a single tear fall. Rémy didn't answer, seeming to just be letting her have her say. Or maybe he just didn't care and was ignoring her. Clearly, she didn't know him at all.

"I'm leaving. Now. Obviously, I can't prevent you from doing...whatever your money will buy, but I'm certain that Charles would never hurt anyone. *I* would never hurt anyone. You do whatever you feel you have to, but I want nothing more to do with you."

She turned to leave, but she paused and half-turned her head. "And, Rémy, all you had to do was ask. I would have told you anything you wanted to know."

As Rémy sat there alone in the alcove long after Annelise had left, he told himself that he'd been right to act the way he had, that it had been necessary to use every advantage that he could in order to get to the bottom of the mysterious attacks on his family, including his prior history with her from Mexico. *I'm the good guy, damn it.* He'd been playing his part in order to find out whatever he could from her, and he'd done it. He'd pretty much cleared Annelise of suspicion, which was good for her, and found out info from her that might lead to the actual culprit or culprits. They'd never given any promises to each other or talked about their futures. He'd made sure of it, knowing that the time would likely come when she'd learn everything, when she'd walk away from him.

Why do I feel so goddamn guilty, then? Like his heart had hurt when he'd seen the tears glittering in her eyes before she'd blinked them away. He'd gone into this knowing that his relationship with her, whatever it was, would likely be collateral damage. He'd believed that he'd be okay with that. But now, when it was too late, he had the creeping sensation that maybe he hadn't been playing a part at all. He'd really enjoyed being with her, as much here as he had in Mexico, maybe even more. He'd stayed on target with his questions, but he hadn't needed to make love to her so many times, to talk to her the way he had, to tell her things he'd never really shared with anyone, not even his brothers. No, all of that had been for him and him alone.

And maybe she was right. *Probably* she was right. He hadn't needed to do most of what he had to get the answers he'd needed. He'd been selfish and used her, long after he'd needed to, because he liked her. He liked her company, liked her smile, and he more than liked the way she gave herself to him, the way it felt to be buried deep inside her. He hadn't wanted that to end.

Now, when it was too late to explain or change his actions, he realized that maybe he was just as much of an ass as she probably thought he was. She'd done nothing to deserve him hurting her, and he should have considered another path to obtaining the information. He felt a hot wave of shame well up in his chest.

He looked down at his phone, realizing to his surprise that he still held it in his hand. And it was vibrating. The message from Villiers made him jump to his feet.

"Another possible lead willing to meet. Call me ASAP for details."

If he'd gotten that message the day before — or even an hour earlier — he would have been thrilled. This could be just the in that they needed. Now, he felt only grim satisfaction. He looked around the small space once more, possibly the last place he would ever see Annelise, still lovely even when she'd been furious, her cheeks rosy and her hair tumbling everywhere. Something inside him actually ached at the memory, squeezing. Feeling heavy, he stood and went quickly to the door of the secret passage and back up to his suite to call Villiers.

Chapter Eleven

Why the hell couldn't the punk kid have chosen a location inside, Rémy wondered, not for the first time since he'd been standing outside freezing his balls off for at least fifteen minutes. If the kid didn't show… He did another slow turn, taking in the deserted appearance of the abandoned warehouse that loomed over the small access road he currently stood in the middle of. It was such a cliché — meeting someone from the underbelly of society at an abandoned factory — but it was also convenient. The police didn't come here often, there were no security cameras, and Villiers had told him that junkies and homeless people had long ago started using the factory as a convenient crash pad, so some activity wasn't totally noticeable, either. Unfortunately, it was an exceptionally cold night, and his contact was late. Just when Rémy had almost given up, he heard a rustling noise. It was slight, though, like someone small.

With their family's vast fortune and influence in the business world, he and his siblings had pretty much always been at risk. Primarily their parents had worried about kidnapping, and so they'd insisted all the children become adept at several different martial arts and also with weapons from a young age. It was non-traditional, and Pierre and Clothilde had never enjoyed it much, but Rémy and Luc had really excelled, Rémy especially. He still practiced at a private club he was a member of as often as he could, and he called now on all of the watchful preparedness that he'd learned over many years. His disappointment and concern were almost palpable when he saw a young girl shuffle out from the shadows.

Correction… Not a young girl but a young woman. As she drew closer, her eyes gave her age away. She probably wasn't more than eighteen or nineteen, but her eyes looked ancient. Weary.

"This is no place you want to be, *petite*," he said in French, but she didn't move.

"You're Gaspard."

His senses went on high alert. So, she wasn't here by accident.

"One of them, yes," he answered.

"Do you have the money?" She shivered, shrinking into herself a little for warmth. Her coat was threadbare, and he felt a welling of sympathy. She was probably being forced into doing this somehow, maybe by a boyfriend or even a drug dealer.

"I do." He lifted the briefcase slightly. It hadn't been easy to get so much cash on such short notice, but his family were some of his bank's top clients, after all. The request had been very specific. One of the Gaspard brothers had to come in person, alone, with an enormous amount of cash in a bag. With Pierre still not at his best and Luc far away, running down leads outside Paris, Rémy was the one who'd made the most sense. Villiers had told him he was being foolish to go totally alone, abiding by the details of the request, but he hadn't wanted to do anything to spook the informant or lose out on whatever information he was willing to share. Rémy was honest enough to admit, internally, that perhaps he wanted to punish himself for the way he'd acted with Annelise and that maybe he felt he had to prove that he could do what was needed to protect his family.

"What's the name I'm looking for? Who is behind all the attacks?" he prodded.

Her eyes darted around nervously and she licked her cracked lips. "He doesn't forgive betrayal. He's crazy…like, totally fucked-up-in-the-head crazy. I think this was a bad idea."

Weirdly, Rémy wasn't sure if she was warning him or herself. They'd had a sense from their investigations that they were dealing with a real expert, one with deep enough pockets to have an inside informant at the police department. The fact that they'd had difficulty finding anyone willing to say anything had indicated that somehow, the culprit inspired loyalty, but they hadn't known how afraid his own people were of him.

"You know, you don't have to do it this way. Just tell me his name and I'll give you the money, but I can also help you, find you someplace to stay, help you get back on your feet."

The girl's smile was cynical and her eyes were hard. "Yeah, buddy. I've heard that one before."

He felt more than saw something falling down onto him from above, and while he didn't have enough time to fully avoid the heavy object, he moved enough to only feel something hard and heavy land a glancing blow to his shoulder. Hot pain lanced through him, and he knew it would be a deep bruise, but he was lucky it hadn't taken his arm right out of its socket. He didn't dare look down, though, because he saw a slight figure disengage from the shadows in the doorway to the building. It was a young man, looking much more like Rémy had pictured the informant—pale, with deep shadows under his eyes, but with a calculating intelligence in his expression. He held a knife and slashed out at Rémy, catching his coat but not cutting him. Rémy dodged and weaved, calling on all of his training, and managed to land a hard jab to the young man's wrist. Just as he'd hoped, it forced the kid to drop his weapon. Before Rémy could pick it up, though, he felt a crushing hit to the side of his head.

It reverberated through his entire body, and his cheek and left eye felt like they might explode. The pain was so intense that it made him suck in a shocked breath, but he pushed it aside to turn to defend himself. The young woman stood, clutching a baseball bat.

"Drop the bag," she said. Through the buzzing in his skull, Rémy still managed to have the presence of mind to keep himself between the pair and the knife, which still lay on the ground. He never took his eyes off the girl as he unstrapped the briefcase from where he'd looped it across his shoulders.

"We won't give you any information," she said loudly, as if she were speaking to someone else in addition to her accomplice and Rémy. Maybe whoever had thrown the object from above? Rémy tasted blood in his mouth and his entire face throbbed. He knew he was fortunate to still be conscious and on his feet.

Rémy raised his hands in a gesture of surrender. It had been a rookie move, not expecting violence from the girl. She looked so young, but clearly, she wasn't averse to jumping into the fray. And now he was under no illusions as to his odds. He was alone in a deserted alley, outnumbered and injured already. Unbidden, Annelise's face flashed before his eyes but not his last memory of her, hurt and furious. No, it was her smile as she'd teased him that night in the hot tub, beckoning him straight to the paradise of her body. *Dieu*, he'd give anything to see that again. He hated that he was going to die with that regret on his conscience, along with knowing that he'd failed his family. But damn it, he wasn't going to go down easy. He braced his legs and held his body tense. Alert. They'd surprised him before, but not again.

"Now go," the girl said. He froze, not understanding at first. Her companion's face looked thunderous.

"Lisette, you can't —"

She glared at the scraggly youth and cut him off. "Get out of here, now," she ordered.

Rémy would have liked to stay and fight, but with any number of unknown attackers, he knew he should take whatever chance he had, the chance that, apparently, the girl was giving him, against the wishes of at least one of the others. With a swiftness that made the world spin and bile rise up in his throat from the pain, he grabbed the knife from the ground before walking as fast as his long legs would carry him, back to where he'd hidden the nondescript older car Villiers had arranged for him to borrow. Every step jarred his head and made his nerves light up with fiery darts of pain, but he pushed on, darting continuous glances around himself to ensure that he wasn't being followed.

Normally, he was relatively confident that he'd come out ahead, no matter whom he met in a dark alley, but tonight it was a struggle to even walk along the city streets. His breathing was labored, and he was seeing spots. He definitely had a head injury of some sort, and he would have a monster shiner and fat lip as well. That was just if he was lucky. When he finally spotted the dull silver of the borrowed compact car, he could have kissed the top of it. Practically panting, he checked the perimeter alarm he'd set up and felt dizzying relief that it hadn't been tripped. Or maybe he was just dizzy. Frankly, he didn't care. He got in and drove away, as fast as he could manage, intent only on getting to the hospital with the private emergency room where they'd previously taken his sister and brother. He was damn grateful to be alive.

Chapter Twelve

"Wait, what? You randomly ran into the French hunk you've been going on and on about since you got back from Mexico, you hooked up with him again on what sounds like the hottest night of your life — I'm reading between the lines here — then you had some huge argument that made you run out of the hotel that he happens to own?" Marina's voice was incredulous and so loud that some of the conversations at the neighboring tables quieted.

"It was a pretty bad argument. I...found out he had been using me for information about... Well, it doesn't really matter. He admitted it. He wasn't even sorry...just said he was doing what he had to for his family."

Marina's brown eyes widened incredulously before she went soft with sympathy and understanding. "Oh, honey, I'm so sorry." She reached across the table and squeezed Annelise's hand. Annelise felt the sting of tears at her friend's warm sympathy.

"Thanks. I don't even know why I'm still thinking about it...about him."

Marina ate a sweet potato fry before she answered. "Because you cared about him. I could tell how much you liked him, after you came back from your trip. God, I'm so sorry he hurt you. *Pendejo*. Was he at least sad about it? He should be. He should regret it until his last breath." She narrowed her eyes in an exaggerated way. "Eduardo and I can make him regret it. You know we can, especially Eduardo."

Annelise smiled in spite of herself at Marina's bloodthirsty tone. Eduardo, her brother and an elite ex-special-forces operative, probably could follow through on her threats, though of course her friend had been joking.

She considered Marina's question before she answered. "Actually, he did look like he felt crappy about it...what he'd felt he had to do."

Marina nodded emphatically. "As he should have. How did you leave things with him?"

Annelise swirled her straw around the ice in her cup. "I told him I didn't want anything more to do with him. And apparently he believed me, because I definitely haven't heard from him."

Marina paused with her next fry halfway to her mouth. "Did you want to?"

Annelise shrugged. Yeah, if she were honest, she'd wanted to hear something. She'd told herself that it was so she could hang up on him or slam the door in his face, but some secret part of her had hoped for a real apology. Groveling. Anything to show he'd actually cared.

"I think I really did," she admitted softly.

Marina's eyes were warm with sympathy. "Then maybe you still will," she suggested.

Annelise forced a smile she didn't entirely feel. "He'd better not call now... I spent the whole weekend telling my cat what a rat bastard he is."

"Well, luckily Penelope can't tell him what you said." Marina laughed. "Are you going to eat the rest of your fries?"

"Go ahead," Annelise answered, waving her hand toward her nearly full plate. "I don't have too much of an appetite."

"I'm sorry I wasn't here."

Annelise shook her head. "Oh my God, don't be sorry. You were where you needed to be. I hope you gave your nana my best." She didn't know how her closest friend managed to look so stylish even while she devoured the extra French fries, but it was an undeniable skill.

"I did, and she sent back lots of hugs and kisses. She misses you, loves you...all that good stuff." Even talking with a mouth full of potatoes, Marina was elegant. Life really wasn't fair.

Then Marina narrowed her eyes. "But don't think you're going to change the subject. I want to hear about everything, every last, juicy detail. I'm living vicariously through you now that I've decided to pursue a life of celibacy."

Annelise rolled her eyes. "You know you can have almost anyone you want, right? You know you're gorgeous, and smart and funny..."

"And now you sound like my nana! Only you'd have to say —"

"*Smile, mija! You look so pretty when you smile.*" The two women broke off into giggles as they repeated

Marina's grandmother's favorite phrase in unison. Marina's face grew serious.

"I couldn't have anyone, you know."

Annelise covered her friend's hand in instant sympathy. "I know… I didn't mean to make you sad, Rina."

Marina shook her head and smiled, but it looked forced now. Annelise hated that she'd inadvertently reminded her friend of the love of her young life. Jaime had died a long time ago, but she knew the pain was still very deep. Marina had never seriously dated anyone else, despite trying a few times.

Marina looked down at her watch and frowned in dismay. "Shoot, I told the Dragon I'd be back by two. She'll be watching for me." The Dragon was Marina's more senior colleague, and the head of the resource center at the large consulting firm where she worked. The Dragon — otherwise known as Darlene — also hated Marina. Annelise had seen it herself any time she had visited Marina at work, which was rare.

"Go!" she urged. "We'll talk later. I already feel better. We can hash out a plan next time to help me meet a hunky Scottish bagpipe player. You know I've always loved kilts."

"Ooh, me too!" Marina returned, gathering her phone and purse and taking several bills out of her wallet.

"No…I've got this." Annelise waved her off. "It's the least I can do for the free therapy."

Marina laughed again and put the money back into her purse. "Ok, I'll let you, but I'll buy the cocktails tonight, then. Bruno's?" She named one of the trendier bars nearby.

Annelise nodded. "Fancy cheese appetizers and overpriced drinks that could put hair on the chest of a sailor? Count me in," she deadpanned.

Marina snorted. A ladylike snort, but a snort all the same, and Annelise couldn't contain her blast of laughter.

"You're too much!" her friend said through her laughter.

"I know. That's why you love me. Now go, or the Dragon will be breathing real fire." Annelise waved at her friend.

"Okay, see you later!" Marina turned and glided out of the dining room, leaving a waft of her signature perfume in her wake and turning the heads of most of the men as well.

Annelise was still smiling when she paid the check. Looking at her own watch, she decided she had enough time for a walk through the Public Garden before she went back. She seldom took lunch, much less a long lunch, but today was a particularly light day, with Charles leaving early. Instead of turning back to the office, she turned toward the beckoning green park, surrounded by a wrought-iron fence. It amazed her every time how peaceful it felt, right in the middle of downtown Boston.

It had been growing pretty cool at night, but now, in the bright late-autumn sunshine, the air felt pleasantly crisp. The last vibrant leaves still clung to the trees, and the sound of the water in the pond was soothing. Unerringly, her feet carried her past all of the trees and the pond to the sculptures. She'd always loved to see such beauty on display for everyone. She sat in front of one of her favorites, relaxing, when she suddenly felt a warm glow. She didn't know if it was a sound or even a hint of a smell on the air, but she turned and almost did a double-take when she saw the figure behind her.

"Rémy?" she asked, incredulous.

He was as tall as ever, stylish in a gray overcoat made of a finely-cut and fitted wool, a blue scarf she was sure must be cashmere looped around his neck in the European way, and his hands covered in black leather gloves. His hair was slightly windblown, giving him a rakish look.

"Good surprise or bad surprise?" he asked. His tone was carefully light, but she could hear real uncertainty behind his words. As he spoke, she noticed his lip looked red and a little puffy and one eye was surrounded by swollen, purple skin. In fact, his whole cheek looked swollen.

"You're hurt!" she exclaimed, forgetting to feel awkward as she rushed toward him, standing on her tiptoes to examine his face and touching his cheek softly. She snatched her hand away when he winced. "Oh my God, are your brothers and sister all right?"

The expression on Rémy's face was surprised, then tender. "You have such a beautiful heart, *chérie*. My siblings are fine. And I'll be all right too. It looks worse than it really is. My lip doesn't actually hurt much." He shook his head as if to dismiss her concern. Then he quirked his mouth into a crooked smile. "Although if I had known that this was all I had to do to get you to run to me, I would have let the other guy hit me harder."

Annelise froze, realizing what she'd done, how close she stood to him, how good he smelled — and looked, and...everything. She'd temporarily forgotten her anger and deep hurt in her concern, but now it came back in full force and her cheeks turned hot with a mix of embarrassment and fury.

She started to look down, but felt Rémy's cool, leather-covered finger gently on her chin.

"Please, *bébé*. I beg you. Please just give me a chance to say something. Then you can walk away again if you want to... I should have said this before." His voice, heavy with yearning and contrition, made her look up again into his beautiful eyes, which were dark with concern and honesty.

Now was the moment of truth. Would she make the leap from hoping he would call so she could hang up on him to listening to whatever he had to say? She bit her lip, considering, but she thought she already knew the answer. She'd learned the hard way how quickly life could change. Joy could transform to anguish. People made mistakes. And she wouldn't be able to sleep, wondering what he might have said. She'd hear him out.

"I don't know if I can ever forgive you," she warned.

He nodded.

"But I'll listen to whatever you want to say."

The whoosh of breath that escaped him was undeniably relieved. "*Merci, bon Dieu*," he breathed. "I thought I would find you furious, refusing to see me. But instead, I find hope."

Annelise scowled. "Don't get ahead of yourself, bud. I only said I'd listen. You really hurt me." She hated that she heard a catch in her voice.

"I know." His voice was heavy, weighted with remorse. "And I believe it will always be my greatest regret."

She looked up and held his gaze. In spite of his injuries, he was so handsome, standing there in front of her with his hair blowing, right in the middle of the Public Garden with the harvest-colored trees and green bushes behind him, surrounded by a stunning clear blue sky. His expression was pained. Rémy, always so proud and confident, bossy even, looked harrowed, as if he'd truly agonized over how things had gone.

She inclined her head, just a little bit, but he took it for the softening that it was.

"You were right. I was utterly wrong to treat you the way I did, to use your generosity and passion for myself. I know that now. But worse than the way I acted with you was that I truly didn't understand why it was wrong. No excuse I can offer really makes up for that. I was an arrogant ass. I think it was just easier to tell myself that I suspected you, even when some part of me knew that you weren't involved, because I'm so used to people wanting something from me...power, influence, money. Even when I've tried to get away from it, by teaching and traveling, restoring buildings, it's always been there because it's a part of me." He rubbed his hand on the back of his neck, wincing. "It was easier to believe that you were pretending with me than that I'd really felt such an instant draw to you."

Annelise was silent, thinking over what he'd said. The park was quiet. It was too late in the season for most tourists, and too early for most commuters. She could hear the soft swish-swishing of the water from the pond. Rémy stood perfectly still.

She still wasn't sure if she could get beyond the hurt, but she realized that she might be beginning to forgive him. What he said made sense. With his background, he probably had a hard time believing in people, especially with how his sister's boyfriend had hurt her, someone he'd said they'd considered family. And she had the creeping realization that she might have been so quick to totally dismiss what he'd done because she, too, was still leery of trusting too much, too far. She'd told herself she was putting herself out there entirely, but had she been? It was definitely his fault, but she thought maybe she could understand.

"I appreciate that you came to explain," she finally answered. Rémy's face fell and he nodded.

"I didn't come with any expectation," he answered.

Honesty made her add, "And maybe—but no promises—it might be a tiny bit understandable, even though you were totally wrong. I've thought about it a lot, and I can't imagine how scary it must be to have some unknown person after your family, hurting your brother and sister. It might make anyone a little crazy."

He visibly relaxed his shoulders. "No matter what, thank you for that, my Annelise," he said softly.

"What made you decide to come?" she asked. Then with more concern, she touched the skin near his bruise again, this time with featherlight fingers, "And what happened to you?"

Rémy's wry half-smile was a shadow of his usual grin. "Something that does not make me look very good, but I don't want any more secrets between us. Want to sit?" He motioned toward one of the benches.

She nodded, and after she'd sat, he settled close next to her, so naturally that she thought maybe it hadn't even been on purpose. She turned into him slightly, too. It hadn't been that long, but she'd missed him, the feel of him. She couldn't help herself from wanting to be closer.

Annelise drew her eyebrows together. "Was it a fight? Or some sort of attack?"

Rémy tilted his head. "You could say that. I, ah, met with someone who said he would tell us who was behind the attacks...for a price."

"What?" she gasped. "You mean, the police let you come along?"

Rémy looked abashed. "No police. I went alone. And...it was a bit of a setup, I'm afraid. But I'm tougher than I look."

Annelise thought of his hard muscles, which she knew were lean and toned under his clothing. She would bet they had been in for a surprise if they'd attacked Rémy. But still... "How could you? You could have been hurt. You *were* hurt! Oh my God, you could have been killed!"

He laid one hand over hers lightly. "It was, well... In hindsight, I may have done things differently. But I couldn't let the chance pass us by. With him still out there, everywhere we go, we're worried, just waiting to see what will happen next. He seems to have more information than he possibly should know."

He squeezed her hand and looked away as he spoke again. "When things looked...bad, I thought of you, *bébé*. How beautiful you look when you hold me inside you, lovelier than anything I've ever seen before. And I hated that I might never see you again to tell you I was wrong and that I was sorry — so sorry I hurt you."

In the silence that followed, Annelise's mind reeled. The enormity of what she'd almost lost had just hit her. She'd left Rémy, the man she now realized she might have very deep feelings for, and he'd almost been killed. He could have died without them ever speaking again, too hurt to try to get beyond one big mistake. Life was too short to hold on to all the fear and past pain, and she vowed in that instant to let go of it enough to give them another chance. They both deserved to see where their passionate connection and growing feelings might lead. The alternative of losing him out of fear of getting hurt again was unthinkable.

"How did they hurt your face?" she asked in a small voice.

He looked reluctant, but he answered. She could swear she saw a dull red flush rise on his cheekbones. "Ah, a baseball bat, actually."

"Oh my God, Rémy! A baseball bat?"

"I wasn't expecting it from such a small woman. I should have known better. It's been a long time since someone got the drop on me like that."

"Rémy, I…don't know what to say." Annelise's voice cracked, and she tried not to give in to the tears that suddenly threatened.

Rémy slowly put his arm around her and stroked her hair. "*Non, chérie*. Please. I can't stand to see you cry. It's over, and I'm all right. It was *stupide*, arrogant to go alone, no matter my reasons."

He held her for a long moment and they both seemed to take comfort from the embrace. He was warm and solid, and she reminded herself that he was there. No matter what, she had this moment with him.

"Would you have been so sad to never see me again?" he asked. The teasing note was back in his voice, but she thought she heard something else, too.

She looked up at him and held his gaze with her own. She took a deep breath. "Yes," she answered baldly. "Yes, I would have."

"*Bébé*, you don't know how much I love to hear you say that. I would have traveled many more miles and gone through almost anything for that look from you."

His mention of travel jogged her memory and she looked around, noting that the sun had gone behind a cloud and she hadn't even noticed. "What time is it? Shoot... I might be late for the one meeting I do have."

"Ah, so sorry, *chérie*. The young lady at your office told me your three o'clock meeting was canceled. Your colleague had to leave early. I meant to tell you but when I saw you...it took other thoughts right out of my head."

Annelise smiled and shook her head at his outrageous flirtation. "You spoke with Sam?"

Rémy nodded. "When I didn't find you at your office, I asked around to see what I could find out about your whereabouts. She saw me and came out to greet me. She was very...forthcoming. She told me where you'd gone and about your schedule."

"I'll bet she was," Annelise answered. Sam was someone she considered to be a friend, but she was also notoriously chatty—and especially friendly to a handsome man.

In fact, she was surprised that Sam hadn't texted her or something. The thought made her realize she hadn't checked her cell phone since lunch, and when she pulled it out and glanced at the screen, she couldn't help a snort of amusement.

There was a message from Sam.

Yum. You can thank me later. Don't come back. I wouldn't. Roger's gone for the afternoon anyway.

Roger was their other supervisor and the only person apart from her colleague who'd apparently had to leave who would have possibly been looking for her that afternoon. It seemed the universe might be conspiring to give her some time with Rémy smack dab in the middle of a Monday afternoon.

"Yum?" Rémy asked, his voice rumbling close to her ear as he read over her shoulder.

"Hey! Eavesdroppers never hear anything good about themselves," she scolded.

"Don't they?" He quirked up one dark eyebrow and she could have sworn her heart started to beat erratically.

"She's…not wrong," Annelise conceded.

"That's the best you can do?" Rémy teased, moving closer and tucking her hair behind one ear.

"You know how sexy you are. You don't need me to tell you," Annelise answered, her voice growing suspiciously husky. The day, which had been feeling a little cool, now felt blazing hot.

"Oh, but I like hearing you say it. Hearing naughty words come out of your sexy little mouth with your pretty, pink lips. You're delicious, *chérie*." He kissed her, and it felt as natural as breathing. She just sort of melted into him as he stroked his tongue into her mouth, taking his time, tasting her lips. He put his arms fully around her and she smelled his warm, spicy male scent. This time, she admitted, it was like coming home.

When he finally lifted his head and broke the kiss, they were both a little breathless.

"I dreamed of that, my Annelise. Every hour we were apart I wondered if I'd ever get to do that again. I don't know how I found you — how we managed to find each other — but damn, I won't give up easily. It's crazy… I know it's crazy, but you're special. Different. I hope — I hope you think we're worth a chance?"

For the second time since she'd met Rémy, Annelise felt like her heart took control of her words before she could even form them. "Come home with me, Rémy, and I'll show you how I feel."

It was impetuous—brazen, even. It was broad daylight in the middle of a park, for heaven's sake, and there was still a lot to be resolved between them, but she wasn't sorry. She would risk that and much, much more if it meant Rémy might be the prize at the end of the game.

His eyes widened in surprise for a split second then darkened with desire and…something deeper. Maybe tenderness, and—she hoped she read him correctly—affection? He pulled her closer than she'd realized she could be with all their clothes on, so she could feel his hard muscles, even through the layers of fabric that separated them. He grabbed both of her coat lapels, brushing his long, strong fingers over her nipples as he did so, making them bead into tight little peaks. Without warning, he pulled her deftly right up onto his lap, and she could feel his hardness pressing against her sex, proof of the magnitude of his desire.

"Anywhere you want me, *bébé*. Any time. I. Am. *Yours*."

She shivered with passion and longing, hearing the intensity and sincerity behind his words.

"Let's take a cab," she said.

Chapter Thirteen

As if by agreement, they didn't speak much on their way to Annelise's apartment. It wasn't far. In fact, she'd normally never indulge in a cab for the quick trip but she couldn't wait a moment longer to be alone with Rémy. Private. The force of her feelings was nearly overwhelming. Shocking. Somehow, she could sense he felt something similar, by the way his hand lingered on her thigh before holding hers and by the sidelong looks he kept slanting her way.

The silence should have felt awkward, but instead it felt intimate and charged with something big. Powerful.

When they pulled up to the front of her building, Rémy's smile was almost predatory. Satisfied.

"Short ride," he remarked.

"It felt too long to me," she answered in a low voice, only for him.

He pulled several bills out of his wallet, handing them to the astonished cabbie without really looking at him.

"It's too much," the man said, but Rémy shook his head, all the while never taking his eyes off of Annelise.

"Keep it."

As they walked up the steps that led into the historic brownstone in Boston's Back Bay neighborhood where her new apartment was, she felt suddenly uneasy. The contrast between the luxury of his penthouse suite and her cozy little one-bedroom in the attic was stark. Rémy put one large, warm hand on her lower back as if sensing her need for reassurance.

"What is it? Not regrets, I hope?"

"I, ah... My place is pretty small." She bit her lip.

The worried frown which had appeared between Rémy's thick, dark brows smoothed and disappeared. "I don't mind, *bébé*. I want to be as close as I can to you, anyway. It's yours, and so I will love it."

Again, his words should have sounded like an exaggeration, but instead...it sounded as if he meant them. *Still...*

"We have to walk up three flights, and there are a few boxes left that I haven't unpacked," she continued, but her concerns were already disappearing. All she could think about was how broad his shoulders were, whether his chest was as muscular as she remembered and how soft and warm his eyes looked right then.

"If you keep looking at me that way, we won't get upstairs before I show you how much I don't care about those things. I'll be forced to show you right here — to kiss you up against this wall then put my hand into your panties to feel how wet I make you."

"Oh my God," she breathed.

"That's the look again. *Bébé*, I can't take it," he growled, and that was all the warning she had before he turned her and pressed her up against the exposed brick wall.

Just like he'd said he would, he slanted his mouth over hers and pressed against her, stroking her everywhere at once with his large, strong hands and possessing her. She could feel the length of his arousal growing long and hard against the softness of her belly. He kissed her until every other thought left her head and all she could think of was his taste, his scent and the feel of him. Her skin and nerves were hypersensitive, craving more and more. When he stepped back, she might have fallen if he hadn't been holding her. That was how much he affected her.

Her heart nearly leaped right out of her chest when she heard someone clear his throat. It was Mr. Mundy, the small elderly man from 2B. "Didn't mean to stop you, but there are children who live in this building." He winked and shuffled past them.

They were both silent until the door closed behind them when they burst out laughing. Annelise laughed so hard that her stomach ached and tears sprang into her eyes. Rémy laughed so that he looked as carefree as the little boy he must have once been.

"Oh my God! How much do you think he saw?" Annelise choked out between bouts of laughter.

Rémy shook his head. "A lot," he managed to answer. "I don't think he minded, though."

"How am I ever going to pass him in the hallway again? I can never leave my apartment!" Annelise wailed.

Rémy's voice grew gruff. "That sounds like a plan. You. Me. In your apartment. Forever. We'll never wear clothes again and order takeout for every meal."

Annelise giggled at the absurdity. "How are we going to pay for it?"

Rémy tapped his chin thoughtfully. "Good question. Slide an envelope under the door? Or hide behind the door? I'll figure it out, as long as I get the radiant beauty of my goddess to myself for eternity." He leaned closer until his warmth surrounded her again. "Yours is a body that should never be covered."

A thrill shot through her, even as she laughed at how silly he was being. She reached around and squeezed his butt. "Ditto, big guy. Let's go upstairs."

As Rémy walked behind Annelise, he fought the urge to squeeze her ass as she'd squeezed his. Part of him was still incredulous. How the hell had he been lucky enough to find her, yet again, and have her maybe forgive him? It felt almost surreal, but in the best possible way. He wasn't under any illusions about what had happened in that alley. He had come within a hair's-breadth of death. If the young woman hadn't mysteriously let him leave, he wouldn't have been able to stop them from killing him. The thought was chilling. He never would have seen his Annelise again, never would have gotten the chance to explain.

In the intervening nights, the majority of which he'd spent traveling alone, he'd had more time to think. One thing had crystallized in his brain. He wasn't sure exactly what he felt for Annelise, but it was deep and real, and while he didn't want to scare her off, he also couldn't stand the idea of not telling her — of something else happening and her not knowing.

He watched her shapely bottom move as she climbed the steps in front of him, and he reflected that, instead of it being a drawback, he rather thought that her apartment being a walk-up was a bonus. *Bon Dieu*, she had a fine ass, especially since he knew what it looked like uncovered. If this wasn't real, and instead of Annelise apparently forgiving him he was only dreaming of her in a hospital bed somewhere, he didn't care. It was worth it.

When they started on the last flight of stairs, he decided he couldn't hold out any longer and he leaned forward, pinching her directly on one luscious buttock. Hard. She yelped and turned around, but when he thought she might scold him, she surprised him by blushing. She *liked* it.

"Not yet, Rémy." His cock, which had been stiff pretty much since he'd seen her, standing in the cool park in front of the sculpture, now went harder than he'd realized it could. He was surprised it didn't just burst out of his trousers. She turned away, giving him another view of her sexy behind, but she turned back again sharply. "My turn next." Her voice was low and husky with arousal. That settled it. She might just be perfect. *Perfect for me, in any case.* He hurried to follow her up her stairs.

When they finally walked into her apartment, he just had time to get the impression of cozy and warmly-colored decorations before she closed the door and he couldn't wait another second to have her in his arms again. She must have had the same idea since she practically threw herself into his embrace, and he backed her against her front door, kissing her lips and face, and dragging his fingers through her silky hair, dislodging the little clip she'd been using to hold her hair half-up. It fell to the ground with a clang, and he kicked it aside.

Her hands were everywhere, too, running through his hair, although carefully avoiding his bruised eye and cheek, molding his broad shoulders and chest. He leaned into her softness, reveling in the contrast between it and his hardness. He groaned as she wiggled against him, brushing his cock with her hip.

"*Bébé*, you're driving me mad," he ground out.

She looked up, lips pink and swollen from his kisses, her hair in complete disarray, and he thought he'd never seen anything so beautiful.

"Good," she whispered, and he took her mouth again. When she began unfastening his coat, he broke their kiss.

"If you keep that up, we won't make it to your bedroom." His voice was so guttural he almost didn't recognize it.

His heart leaped when she turned her blue gaze on him again. "I don't care. I need you, Rémy. Inside me. Right now."

She shrugged off her own coat and shirt in one smooth motion, revealing a lacy black bra covering the creamy fullness of her breasts, and she began to unfasten her pants. Their breathing was loud and harsh in the little entryway, and it took him a second to recover from the bolt of arousal the sight shot through him. When he realized she was serious, he hurried to catch up. If his woman wanted him in an entryway, she could have him. Hell, she could have him in the middle of Penn Station.

He shed his own overcoat and suit coat, and he'd started on his shirt when her warm hands stopped him. Her look was glazed with arousal, and she now wore only her bra. His cock pulsed with need as he saw the little thatch of hair covering her mound. She was ready and eager, it seemed.

"Just take off your pants. I want you inside me so badly, Rémy."

With hands that shook a little, he managed to unfasten his pants and push them down, along with his underwear, before he lifted her up against the wall. Her scent was warm and spicy, with the hint of vanilla, and he breathed it in deeply.

She wrapped her arms around him, kissing his shoulders and neck, everywhere she could reach. "I'm so empty. I *need* you," she pleaded, and it was so sexy he almost missed what she whispered next. "You could have *died*."

Now he understood her urgency and he shared it. He hated that he'd done this to her, but on the other hand, he was damn grateful he'd made it through alive so he could be with her again.

"I didn't, *chérie*. I came back to you," he grunted before he thrust into her in a long, hard stroke. She felt like heaven, hot and tight, slick with arousal. She screamed as he seated himself fully, and her pussy rippled around his cock like a velvet fist, making him groan again.

When he'd been traveling, he'd planned—well, hoped, really, because he'd been pretty uncertain whether he had much chance of her forgiving him—for a long, romantic session of lovemaking. He'd lick and stroke her, driving her crazy for an hour or two before finally entering her. But this? This exceeded his wildest expectations. It was primal, wild and beyond anything he'd ever imagined.

He couldn't even stop himself from thrusting into her immediately, but the breathy moans and whimpers she made let him know she was enjoying it as he flexed his hips. He held the globes of her spectacular ass with his large hands, squeezing in time with his thrusts, and she clung to him to hold on as his motions grew wilder.

His arousal mounted so quickly that he might have been embarrassed, but her answering motions told him she was getting close to ecstasy, too, so he sped up until he could hear their lovemaking as a rhythmic thumping on the door, punctuated by the wet sounds of her moisture where he was inside her. Suddenly she stiffened and bit his shoulder as her pleasure overtook her, and her inner muscles clamped around him and milked him, as if they wanted to hold him inside. He tried to hold out, but the feeling of her orgasm was too much for him and he thrust in once more with a hoarse shout, stiffening as he shot his hot seed into her in spurts, filling her completely.

She went limp against him and he stood there, panting, holding her for as long as he could. When his muscles began to shake, he slumped down with her still in his arms so they lay on their discarded coats, wrapped in each other's arms. He almost laughed when he realized he still wore his shirt and shoes, with his pants around his ankles, but he just didn't have the energy. Annelise still wore her bra, too, though he must have pushed the lacy cups down at some point, exposing her pink nipples, which were still puckered into little points. He managed to kiss one, eliciting a gasp from her, before he let his head fall back onto the cushion of his thick wool overcoat.

He wasn't sure how long they lay there, spent and replete, but he noticed that the late-afternoon shadows lengthened as they simply held each other until their breathing slowed to normal. It sounded like Annelise went to sleep. When she stirred again, he turned her toward him.

"That was...beyond what I dared to dream. And, *chérie*, I have done a lot of dreaming about you," he murmured.

"Agreed. But mostly I'm so glad you're safe, Rémy," she whispered. Her cheeks were flushed, and her eyes were still drowsy. When she smiled, he felt something clench in the region of his heart.

He grinned when another thought occurred to him. "I wonder if your neighbor was walking by again. I think he probably heard us, if he did."

Annelise gave an embarrassed laugh. "Um, yeah, I guess I was pretty loud."

Rémy gathered her close and kissed the cloud of her hair near his face. "I love the sounds you make, my goddess. You let me know when I'm doing something you like. And I was hardly silent."

"I like everything you do, Rémy. You're...amazing." She spoke quietly, but her words made something warm grow in his chest, and his cock twitched as well.

She must have felt it against her hip. "Oh my God, you're insatiable!"

He pulled her up so he could kiss her again. "Yes. With you, apparently I am. Where's the bedroom, *chérie*? I want the grand tour."

He hadn't actually meant for her to show him around, but when she smiled at him and pulled her sweater back on—and nothing else—he decided maybe he really did want the tour after all. He stood and pulled his pants back up, laughing when he realized he was almost fully dressed again.

She quirked a questioning eyebrow toward him.

"We have some work to do if we want to live the nudist lifestyle," he answered, and she blushed prettily.

The back of his neck prickled with the uncomfortable but unmistakable sensation of being watched, and he swiveled his head around to see a large, fluffy cat giving him a death stare.

"Er…is your cat glaring at me?"

Annelise looked strangely guilty. "Don't worry. She'll be fine. Penelope's just…protective." She gave the cat a quelling look, and the portly feline turned and walked away with what he could have sworn was a flounce. Very funny — but why should he be surprised? The cat was devoted to Annelise, too, and he didn't even live with her. *Yet*, some inner voice added. Didn't live with her *yet*. Oddly, the idea didn't make him as uncomfortable as he'd expected. On the contrary, in fact.

As they stepped into the living room, he noticed several large plastic containers. He remembered she'd mentioned boxes. "Did you just move in?"

She nodded. "Well, about two months ago, but with my work schedule and living alone…a few business trips. It's not too easy to get everything unpacked."

"So…you never lived here with Kyle?" He watched her face carefully and was pleased not to see even a flinch at his name.

"No. After I got back from Mexico, I just couldn't live in the place I'd shared with him anymore. It was probably holding me back, living there with all those memories. I stayed with my closest friend, Marina, for a couple months while I looked for a new place. It was funny. I'd always wanted to live in the Back Bay."

The Back Bay was one of the most historical and affluent neighborhoods of Boston, and he assumed it was where they were right now.

"But Kyle hated it, so we never looked here. I found this place eventually and I absolutely love it. I wish I'd done it sooner."

"Life can be surprising," Rémy said, thinking of the unexpected direction his life had gone in since he'd met Annelise in Mexico.

Annelise nodded, crossing her arms. "Some bad surprises...but some very, very good ones." She didn't look at him as she spoke, but he knew that she referred, at least in some small part, to him. Or he hoped so.

"Should I be flattered?" he asked, kicking himself for how insecure his question sounded, hanging there in the air.

"Yes," she answered simply. "You were a very, very good surprise, and meeting you — our time together — helped me change the direction of my life to one I'm really excited about."

He stepped closer to her and wrapped his arms around her soft, shapely body, kissing her head. "I'm glad," he answered...and meant it.

She stepped away, but it didn't feel like she was pulling away. Instead, he saw unmistakable pride on her face as she gestured with her arm. "This is the living room. I chose different shades of blue everywhere for my decorating scheme. Sort of...beachy, I guess. I used a few pieces I picked up in Mexico, too."

He glanced around appreciatively, fully seeing and absorbing the time and effort she must have put into the space. "It's gorgeous, *chérie*. I especially like the Mayan statue."

"It's fake," she confessed, but her face was flushed with pleasure. "Of course, I can't afford the real thing. But it's well done, and I thought it really tied the room together."

He nodded. "*Absolument*. It does exactly that. My decorator could take some tips from you. You have a great eye."

The next room she showed him was an office, neat and organized, but also somehow serene. Then came the eat-in kitchen and the bathroom, which was very oceanic. She hesitated before the closed door to the last room.

"I don't mind a mess, *bébé*." He'd been trying to make her feel more comfortable, but at his comment she turned a rosy shade of pink and looked away. She seemed nervous, like she was about to reveal something. Damn, he loved watching her blush creep over her fair skin, especially since he knew that she blushed everywhere. His cock grew harder just thinking about it. But...that was always happening around Annelise anyway.

"It isn't messy," she answered, and her hesitant tone piqued his curiosity. He gave her a questioning glance, stepping toward the door, and when she didn't stop him, silently giving him permission, he pushed open the door.

The bedroom before him was a feast for the senses — blue with pops of red everywhere, giving the impression of a sunset on the beach. There were framed pictures of what looked like the beach they had met on, and the bed was enormous and looked to be covered in a satin coverlet and silk sheets. There were mirrors on the closet doors, and there was a sculpture of two naked lovers embracing set on a pedestal table in the corner. It was certainly sensual, verging on erotic, but definitely tasteful.

When he looked over at Annelise, she was blushing a fiery red but he wasn't certain if it was out of shyness or desire. Possibly both. He crossed the floor in two long strides and took her elbows into his hands.

"It's perfect, *chérie*. Beautiful and artistic, sumptuous and a little bit suggestive, just like you."

She looked up at him with eyes that seemed to hold the mysteries of the universe. "That's exactly what I wanted. I...put it all together, but you're the first person I've actually shown it to."

Rémy's heart soared at her words. He was the first...and if he had his way, the only. He never wanted anyone else to get to see this side of her. He wanted it all to himself. "That...pleases me, more than you'll ever know. But I'll try to show you." He almost didn't recognize the deep, rumbling voice as his own.

"I thought of you when I put it together. I dreamed that maybe..." She bit her lip again, and he ached with the need to nibble it, too. "Maybe you'd see it someday."

Her confession was too much for his self-control, and he picked her up, making sure to slide every curve of her against him as he did so. He let her fall onto the massive bed, and when she flashed him just a hint of her moist core, covered by her soft tuft of hair, every muscle in his body felt like it grew taut with desire. "Mine," he growled, before he pounced on top of her.

Chapter Fourteen

Annelise wasn't sure what she'd said, but somehow she'd put Rémy into a frenzy. He settled himself, fully clothed, between her thighs on the bed and the sensation of the rough fabric against her bare skin was shocking — and erotic. He devoured her mouth, making her lips tingle with his soft brushes and harder sucking, and when he tangled his tongue with hers, she moaned.

He half-lifted up so he could pull off her sweater again, then he deftly unfastened and removed her bra, too, leaving her bare everywhere. When he leaned back down, the feel of the smooth, fine fabric of his shirt rubbing against her nipples, which had gone hard, made her cry out and grow warm all over.

"My beautiful. Responsive. Annelise." He grunted the words as he moved against her, and she reveled in the contrast between the smooth satin below her and the hot, hard male on top of her. She could feel his huge, thick member pressing against her core through his pants.

"Yes," she whimpered, throwing her head back as he lowered his head to pull one nipple into his mouth. He rolled her other nipple between his long, powerful fingers until she was squirming against him with her need. When he finally reached down, she could feel how wet she'd grown by how easily his fingers slid into her soaking channel, but she was too far gone with need to care.

"Mmm, still so wet for me. So ready." He sounded appreciative, and she thrust her chest forward brazenly, earning a dark chuckle. "Don't worry. I'm coming back."

Through her haze of desire, she saw him pull off his clothing at record speed and thought she heard a button ping as it hit the radiator. She had the errant thought that she was hell on his clothes before he was back and she couldn't think of anything but how good her large, naked man felt.

Then she caught sight of the bruise on his shoulder and gasped, but for another reason entirely.

"Oh my God, Rémy, your shoulder!"

He stilled and shrugged. "It's a bit tender, but it looks much worse than it is." She hoped so, because it looked pretty darned bad. It was dark purple in the center, outlined with sick shades of green and blue. She touched the pale skin next to it with gentle fingers, and her eyes stung again at the further proof of how much danger he'd been in.

"No, *chérie*. Let me make you forget what might have happened and remember that I'm here now, loving you." Before she could even think about his words, he lowered his head to her chest.

When he'd finished thoroughly licking each nipple, all the while curling two fingers into her, she was practically panting with need. Instead of entering her, though, as she expected, he scooted down the bed and began lapping at her core. She still felt the last vestige of modesty, since it was broad daylight and she was certain he could see everything, but he quickly melted that away with the amazing sensations he was engendering. He licked and stroked inside her with abandon, seeming not to care about how wet she was when it got on his cheeks. In fact, he seemed to revel in it. When he moaned, the vibration of his mouth against her nub was too much and she stiffened and cried out, falling headlong into another orgasm before she'd even realized she was close.

He drew it out, still licking and sucking lazily and stroking one long finger into her until the last quivering echoes subsided. Then he astonished her with his massive strength as he reversed their positions, simply flipping over and lifting her on top of him.

When she gave a shocked gasp at the feel of his swollen sex prodding at her sensitive entrance, he shot her a wicked smile. She turned the tables by sliding onto him, rising up then down again until he filled her with his entire length, touching the very end of her tight channel. She gasped and threw her head back before she started moving over him, rotating her hips and tightening around him. He groaned with pleasure and reached up to squeeze and stroke her breasts. Oddly, she noticed he seemed to be looking over to his left repeatedly. At first, she thought it was nothing, but when it happened again, she turned her head and saw what had captivated his attention.

With the position of the bed and the mirrors, they both had a perfect view of their reflection, naked, making love. Rémy looked gorgeous, of course, but what shocked her was her own reflection. *Can that really be me?* Mesmerized, she looked at the woman in the mirror. She was naked and absolutely comfortable with her curves, flushed with arousal and her lips and nipples were pink and swollen, with a hint of razor burn from Rémy's five-o'clock shadow. Her hair was a tangled mess of silk, but her eyes and her smile were bold, sexy. She was indeed like the goddess Rémy called her.

"Do you see how beautiful you are? How sexy? This is how I see you, always." Annelise tore her eyes away to look down at Rémy. He was handsome, of course, but his gaze was hungry and tender at once.

"Watch yourself, *bébé*. Lift up and see my cock as it goes in and out of you. It's one of the sexiest things I've ever seen."

Annelise hesitated for a split second then she thought, *What the hell?* What did she have to lose? She turned and looked at their reflection as she rose up and down. He was right. It was unbelievably erotic. She could see Rémy's massive cock, the globes of her ass and her breasts jiggling slightly with each movement, the imprints his fingers left on her breasts and her ass as he grabbed them in turns. Best, though, was seeing it all along with the expression of pleasure on his face, so intense that it almost looked agonized. It was magnificent.

Then she had to stop watching because he took over, his thrusts growing frenzied as he grabbed her hips and slammed her down onto his cock until he reached places she was sure she'd never been touched before. She leaned down to steady herself, bringing her breasts closer to his face, and he promptly sucked a nipple inside his hot, wet mouth until she cried out at the riot of sensations.

"Yes, yes, yes," she gasped on every thrust.

"Now, *chérie*. Come for me *now*," Rémy ordered, and amazingly, his words sent her headlong into another waterfall of pleasure that crashed over her, making her shiver and shake as every nerve ending seemed to fire at once.

Rémy tensed below her, too, thrusting up one last time before he stiffened and came with a strangled groan before she felt his warm, silky seed shooting into her.

She collapsed on top of him, with his cock still twitching inside her, and he stroked her hair and back for several long moments while they caught their breath. The sounds of traffic were muted outside, but she guessed it must be full rush hour by now. His chest was slightly sheened with sweat, and she knew her long hair must be a little damp, too, from their exertions, but he didn't seem to care. She peppered kisses on his chest, wherever her mouth could easily reach, and he groaned.

"That feels good."

She felt the deep words as much as she heard them. She kissed his chest again. "I can only kiss your chest, because I can't move," she admitted.

"Good. My master plan worked. Now you're entirely at my mercy." His tone was teasing with an undercurrent of something darker. It sent a delicious tingle down her spine.

She managed to move one boneless arm so she could swirl her finger into his soft chest hair, eliciting what almost sounded like a purr of satisfaction from him.

"What was your plan, actually?"

His expression turned serious. "Honestly, I hadn't thought much beyond that I needed to apologize, and even if you sent me away, I wanted to see you once more, to store up another memory."

How could she keep any distance from him when he said things like that? A wave of tenderness swept over her. Oh yeah, she was in deep. She refused to acknowledge just how deep.

"It's lucky that Charles happened to have a last-minute meeting offsite this afternoon so I could take a long lunch...and never come back!" She laughed, but something tickled at the back of her mind. "It was actually pretty out of character, since he almost always takes me on client meetings—or at least has me put together some talking points, especially since the client asked about me by name. I wasn't paying close attention, but I saw the last sentence of an email when I first walked in. C.R. Vieuxvue. But when I tried to see more from his email—I have access to review, sort and reply on his behalf—it was gone."

Rémy stiffened next to her. "Are you certain that was the name?"

Annelise pulled the covers up over herself, alarmed by his tone. She searched her memory. "Yes, particularly because I'm pretty sure I saw something on Charles' phone once when we were meeting. A text came in from Vieuxvue, and he cut our meeting short. Told me he had to follow up. I don't know why I just remembered. I thought it was strange at the time because Charles is unfailingly polite, especially to me, so it was odd. Do you know this Vieuxvue?"

Rémy sat up, all traces of his earlier languor gone. His face was set in grim lines. "I could be wrong—I actually hope I am—but I suspect it's an alias for the man who I had once hoped to call my brother-in-law. When we were children, Vieuxvue was the name of the kingdom he always pretended he was the king of. Claude, Luc and Clothilde used to play for hours on end." He pulled on his pants with quick, harsh motions. "*Putain de merde*, why didn't my family and I think of this before? So much led to your company, but we'd already dismissed Claude, so we never thought to connect him."

A hard lump of dread lodged in Annelise's stomach. "Do you think Charles is in danger?"

Rémy paused and held her gaze, and his eyes were grave. "I think he may be. And what's more, I think maybe he suspected something. That's why he didn't take you with him."

Annelise stood up and went to where she'd thrown her purse, grabbing her phone then pulling on her shirt from the floor. She called Charles but it went straight to voicemail. She sent a quick text, too.

Spoke to Joan. Time-sensitive question. Pls call me as soon as you can.

Joan was the main contact at their second-largest client, and Charles would never ignore a question from her.

Rémy came out of the bedroom, holding his shirt. His face wore a questioning expression.

Annelise shook her head. "Nothing. He sometimes can't answer me in meetings, but he didn't even text back. He almost always acknowledges anything urgent. We have an understanding that I don't bother him unless it's truly important that he handle it directly."

"*Merde, merde, merde!*" His voice was a frustrated growl. Rémy pulled on his shirt and scrubbed his hand down his face. "I...*we* all suspected Claude was angry, and since things ended between him and Clothilde, I think, well, we noticed he was acting erratically. Mercurial. He seemed furious, beyond a reasonable amount, but...we've known him since he was a small child. Clothilde *loved* him. She was engaged to him, for God's sake. I think...maybe we didn't *want* to see how strange his behavior had actually become. But, *chérie*" — he touched her cheek softly — "now that I think about that behavior more objectively, I fear he may be unstable. I hope to God I'm wrong, but if I'm not... We need to figure this out right away. Do you know where they were meeting?"

Annelise's mind raced, trying to remember some hint or clue, but nothing came to mind. She pictured Charles going alone into a situation to protect her. How like him — and how foolish. How long had he been gone? It must have been at least five or six hours now. Charles was so intelligent in many ways but so foolish in others. Somehow that thought jogged her memory and her eyes widened.

"I don't know where they were supposed to meet, but I'm pretty sure I can find out where they are now...fast." She led Rémy into her office and quickly logged into her work computer, thankful that she'd set it up so she didn't even have to have her work laptop. She could still access a remote desktop from her personal computer. And there, just as she remembered so helpfully downloading after the third time Charles had absent-mindedly misplaced his phone and she'd had to retrace his steps one by one until she found it, was the program that allowed her to locate Charles' phone anywhere in cell range.

"Yes!" she breathed, and she felt Rémy behind her, large and reassuring.

"*Bébé*, you are a genius. And have I mentioned that you must be a truly exceptional executive assistant? I'm impressed."

She didn't react, but she felt a warm glow. It was short-lived, though, as she remembered that Charles was with someone who had potentially been attacking and trying to kill Rémy's family. Had been with him possibly for hours.

She opened the program and clicked to run the search, drumming her fingers impatiently as a little progress wheel spun in the middle of her screen. A red dot blinked and the map zoomed closer and closer, narrowing in on first a particular neighborhood, then a particular street. At last it stopped, and she made a sound of surprise.

"That's only a couple of blocks away. It looks like a historic brownstone. Those can be unoccupied a surprising amount of time because they're frequently being renovated."

"Let's go then."

Annelise gasped. "Aren't we going to call the police?"

Rémy shrugged. "What would we tell them? I'll call Marc. He's my driver-security guard, and I'm sure he's nearby somewhere. Once we confirm what's happening, we can call them."

She touched his bruised cheek gently. "Should we really be following your lead?"

His bark of laughter was genuine. "*Touché, chérie.* But...I'm worried to leave your boss more than we have to. Perhaps we'll discover it's just a regular client meeting, but if not, then every minute might be important. We can be careful and just scope things out for now."

Annelise was nervous but determined. She nodded swiftly. "All right, that makes sense. Then we call the police as soon as we confirm there's something going on."

With the setting sun filtering through the curtains behind him, his face looked older, the craggy lines of his chin and nose more pronounced. He looked like a warrior. He nodded again. "Lead the way, *bébé*."

They pulled on the rest of their things, the majority of which they'd left crumpled by the door in their earlier haste, and they went outside and into the lengthening shadows of the early evening. The streets were much more crowded now, with people hurrying in all directions to get to trains and buses, commuting home. Under other circumstances, it would have been lovely to walk down the picturesque historic streets on Rémy's arm, admiring the architecture. She hoped they'd do that someday.

At the most inconvenient time, a realization hit her with a jolt, and refused to be ignored. Annelise hoped they would be able to do all sorts of things together because she wanted to be with him…always. She'd been so careful to only focus on her anger at Rémy. Even earlier in the afternoon, when he'd been explaining, she'd only focused on the facts — what had been going on, why he had acted the way he had. Then she'd given herself up to physical sensations — the exquisite and unparalleled pleasure of being with Rémy again. She'd utterly ignored her emotions, pushing them aside, maybe even unconsciously, to protect herself from being hurt again.

But now, as they headed into an unknown situation, possibly an extremely dangerous one, honesty forced her to admit that she cared deeply for the man beside her. It had meant an enormous amount to her that he'd come to apologize, and their connection was just as strong, if not stronger, than before. Rémy teasing and laughing was ridiculously appealing, but Rémy honest and genuine as he bared his soul? That Rémy was irresistible.

Holding his hand right there in the street, people hurrying past within inches of them, it hit her. Hard. *I love him.* She wanted to work through whatever they'd have to because she wanted to be with him. The thought was stunning—and exhilarating—but close behind it came the concern that he might not feel the same way. Or that even if he did, it would be too difficult with them living such different lives, in different countries. She was still deciding what to do, if anything, when they approached the final block where the brownstone was—where Charles' phone and hopefully the man himself were.

Annelise seemed unusually quiet as they walked, and Rémy thought she must be anxious. He was anxious too, and even more so because she was with him. He truly hoped that they would just find some sort of secret client meeting, but he feared and expected that they would discover something else, something more sinister. He'd made many mistakes in his life, especially with Annelise, but not digging deeper once they'd initially ruled Claude out had been a whopper. He should have listened more to his gut—and to Annelise—when she'd talked about Charles and how unlikely he was to be involved. They'd focused so much on digging into how Charles was connected that they'd missed what had been staring them in their faces.

How many times was Claude going to hurt his family? He'd already devastated Clothilde with his betrayal, and now it seemed likely that he'd tried to kill them. But why? Out of revenge? They weren't happy with him, sure, but they hadn't sabotaged him in any way. They'd comported themselves with dignity and carried on, separating themselves from him but not doing anything more. Claude had once been their friend. Their fathers had been friends. It baffled him.

He glanced down at his phone, noting with satisfaction that Marc should be meeting them any minute, too. In fact, his security guard, who was acting as his driver on this trip, might even beat them there. It had been unusual that Marc should request to go with him, particularly since they'd fallen into a routine where the guard typically stayed close to Clothilde. She said she hated it and complained bitterly, but Rémy suspected she secretly liked the stoic American. But he'd agreed with no questions when Marc had said he'd wanted to come to Boston, near where he was originally from, if Rémy remembered correctly, and he was damn grateful at the moment that Marc would have their backs. Rémy tensed when Annelise drew in a sharp breath.

"Getting close?" he asked.

She nodded, her glance darting to an unremarkable house halfway down the block with some scaffolding on one side. It wasn't obviously unoccupied, but it certainly might be, depending on how much work they were doing. If it was a setup, it was a brilliant choice, since it was totally believable that a client would want to meet here. Rémy cursed under his breath. The only good thing was that, now they were off the main road, it was pretty quiet on the narrow, hilly side-streets, with very few passersby.

"That's Charles' car across the street, with an orange parking ticket on it. He's been here a while."

Rémy's lips tightened. *Merde, alors.* He studied the building. It looked like so many others—not too tall, slightly ornate molding, a brass plate with some sort of historical fact on it. Normally, he would have been reading all the plaques, but now he just prayed that everything on the inside was as unassuming as the exterior.

He paused and Annelise stopped too, turning to him expectantly.

She was so lovely, there in the last dying rays of the sun, that it took his breath for a second. She looked like she had the first time he'd seen her on that deserted beach in Mexico. It felt like a hundred years ago, but even in a hundred years, he knew he'd never get enough of looking at her. Her lips and cheeks were rosy, her hair fell in wild waves and her eyes were dark with sympathy and concern, in spite of her understandable fear. Her chin was tilted up and her shoulders back, undaunted. Her beauty wasn't only on the outside. She'd proven over and over that she was smart, funny, resourceful, loyal and sexy as all hell. His chest swelled, full of affection for her...more than affection. How could he think to lead her into possible danger like this?

"Why are you looking at me like that? Rémy, I hate to admit it, but you're scaring me a little."

He tucked one lock of her hair, still a little messy from their earlier lovemaking, behind her ear. "Would you consider staying here? Outside, where I'll know you're safe?"

Her expression grew even more determined, just as he'd expected. His goddess. But he'd had to try.

"If I asked you the same question, what would your answer be?"

She had a point. *Damn.*

As he opened his mouth to reply, he noticed something moving fast out of the corner of his eye, and his body went on high alert, every nerve ending coming to attention. Not something...someone, a young man who held the distinct dark form of a gun.

Without thought, Rémy pushed Annelise behind him and yelled something. He wasn't sure what, but he thought it was "Get down!" in English or French.

Just as the young man raised his arm straight out and Rémy braced for impact, he heard the squealing of tires and a loud thump-thump as a large black sedan veered from the road right up onto the sidewalk.

He twisted and somehow managed to tackle Annelise to the ground, taking most of the impact on his back and shoulder. He felt the pain, but distantly, totally focused on getting them to safety. He'd heard two shots ring out.

He took stock of himself, quickly cataloging each body part. He was sore but he was reasonably confident he hadn't been shot. He was pretty sure the shots had come after he'd tackled Annelise. He craned his neck, bracing for whatever came next. When Marc emerged slowly from the car, careful to stay low to the ground and behind the car, Rémy's relief was palpable.

"Bullet-proof glass," Marc offered, nodding tersely at Annelise. "The kid with the gun is definitely down, but we should stay low, close to the car."

"Okay, *bébé*?" Rémy hated that her face looked chalky, her eyes huge. But his Annelise was made of strong stuff. She raised her chin.

"I think so," she answered.

Rémy let out a breath he hadn't known he'd been holding. *Merci Dieu.* "Let's crawl to the car, then, until we know what's going on. You stay here, and Marc and I can go in to check on Charles."

Annelise looked like she was about to protest when they all heard the sound of police sirens approaching rapidly. Rémy figured that made sense. They hadn't had a chance to call yet, but you couldn't shoot at someone in a neighborhood like Boston's Beacon Hill and have it go unnoticed. He pulled Annelise along with him toward the cover offered by the car, and he was impressed at how she remembered to stay low, in spite of how harsh the brick sidewalk must have been on her hands and knees.

They'd just gotten into place when two police cars flew down the narrow street and stopped behind them, blocking off the street. Before they could even respond, they heard a slight sound from the front door of the building.

A voice that Rémy barely recognized as Charles' rang out, wavering at first then growing stronger. "Please don't shoot. My name is Charles Pinkston and I'm unarmed. The man who was holding me is letting me go. I'm coming out with my hands up."

Rémy heard Annelise's sharp intake of breath, and he took her hand and squeezed it. He saw the sheen of tears in her eyes.

"Come out slowly with your hands raised then drop to the ground, arms and legs spread."

There was a tense moment as Charles pushed the door open. He looked haggard and a bit rough around the edges—not the normally urbane man Rémy had become used to seeing in Montreal—but his movements were steady. Charles obeyed their directions, keeping his motions slow and dropping to the ground as soon as he'd cleared the door.

Rémy spoke in a low, calm voice, but one that should carry. "The young man down over there has a gun. We believe he's unconscious, but he was certainly armed. And we suspect that there is another man still inside, possibly armed as well."

The officer nearest to him acknowledged the statement and said something into his earpiece, then a group of officers mobilized toward both the downed shooter and Charles. More cars were arriving every second, and soon there was a veritable army of police officers, along with a fire truck and two ambulances. Rémy marveled that so many vehicles could fit on such a narrow street.

He noticed that several officers remained positioned in a way that he recognized from his own study of martial arts and historical military strategy. They were covering Marc, Annelise and him, watching their every movement for signs that they were armed. He hoped Annelise didn't notice that.

After they had secured Charles and moved him back to the cover of their cars, Rémy saw that they also motioned for two EMTs to come closer to the young man. Rémy hoped the kid wasn't injured too badly to give information, although he felt a hot rage fill him at the fact that the youth had nearly shot them, nearly shot Annelise.

The officers began to approach them slowly, too, and Marc exchanged a significant glance with Rémy. Rémy knew Marc had been in the American military before he'd come to work for the Gaspard family, recommended on the highest authority, and he also knew that his driver-cum-security guard had extensive training. Rémy had never asked for any more details than what had been vetted with their extremely thorough background check and his own sense from Marc that he didn't want to talk about his past. Now, the man moved carefully, with slow, limited motions, speaking in the same calm sort of voice that Rémy had used.

"My name is Marc Constantin, and I work for Rémy Gaspard here. This is his friend, Annelise Simpkins. We're unarmed, but I did hit the young man with my car before he could shoot Mr. Gaspard and Ms. Simpkins. I'm going to reach for my I.D. in my upper left coat pocket."

The tension around them ratcheted up as Marc moved to do what he'd said, then very carefully took his wallet out of his coat, keeping his motions slow. He held it up and continued. "I can toss it to the space between us, and you can verify my name. You'll also see my military I.D. and permit to carry a concealed weapon."

There was another bad moment when Rémy could practically see the police officers holding themselves back, but Marc acted as though he were totally unaffected by the danger. After he'd slowly tossed his wallet, one officer darted forward and reviewed it. He said something quietly into his earpiece and the tension decreased visibly in the set of the shoulders of the other officers present. When the same police officer spoke, his tone was nicer, almost friendly.

"Thanks. I thought I recognized your name from somewhere. Local hero, aren't you?" The police officer's Boston accent was thick, and he pronounced it 'yah name'. "We still have to check you all thoroughly, though."

"Of course," Marc answered, nodding to Rémy and Annelise.

"We understand," Rémy echoed, squeezing Annelise's hand again. He saw from her eyes that she understood. They needed to stay totally calm and cooperative.

He let go of her hand and they stood slowly with their arms raised, to be seized by the police officers.

The next few minutes were a blur of activity, with police officers and other emergency personnel everywhere. Annelise was patted down efficiently and she saw from the corner of her eye that Marc and Rémy were getting the same treatment. When it seemed like they had at least finished their initial search of her and were just starting to ask her questions, she noticed that several officers came from the house, looking disappointed.

"No sign of the captor," one of them confirmed. "He must have fled when he sent out the hostage."

Then she saw Charles, looking much older than his years and a little green around the gills, but he still managed a small smile.

She hurried over, though the officer who'd been questioning her followed closely, protesting. She put a tentative hand on his shoulder.

"Are you all right? Charles, what happened? Why did you come alone?"

His smile was fatherly. "That's a lot of questions. I'm fine and you're fine, which is all that matters. I was foolish, and by the time I began to suspect that something wasn't right, it was too late. I'm only grateful that some instinct told me to keep you out of it, which he wasn't very happy about — "

The officer with Charles interrupted him, gently guiding him toward the ambulances instead. "I'm sorry, ma'am. He's headed for the hospital. It seems like the stress hasn't been good for his heart and he needs to be monitored closely. You'll have to see him there."

Her heart fell. Poor Charles. And she felt a crushing guilt. Had Charles only been involved because of her? His face did look a little ashy, with fine lines she'd never noticed around his eyes and mouth. He didn't deserve any more challenges or sadness. He'd faced enough.

She nodded her understanding, but her lip trembled, even as she tried to still it. Then Rémy was there next to her, warm and solid, holding her up and making her feel stronger, even as they put Charles into one of the ambulances.

"It's all right, *bébé*. He should be all right. It's just for safety. I caught him a moment ago too and he was just worried about you. I guess Claude expected him to tell you where he was going and was furious that he hadn't. He somehow knew I was planning to be with you, which means we still have a serious information leak problem somewhere."

One of the officers with her cleared his throat, and Rémy stepped back slightly, no longer holding her so closely.

"Ms. Simpkins still needs to answer some questions," he said.

"Of course," Rémy answered in his deep voice, confident and assured. "But could we sit down for a minute?"

To her surprise and gratitude, because she was starting to feel fatigue creeping over her, the officers agreed...and before she knew it she found herself sitting on the buttery leather seats of the car. Amazingly, in spite of being driven onto a brick sidewalk, ramming an armed man, then taking two bullets, the car was totally fine. There were two little dents from the bullets, but the paint had barely been scratched.

She'd already felt better, seeing the young man taken away for medical treatment and hearing that Claude was definitely gone, but once they sat down in the back of the car, she felt more of the residual tension seep out of her body. In fact, she began to shake a little bit, and Rémy looked down at her in concern.

"Are you sure you're all right?"

She gave him a tremulous smile. "I...think maybe my body just realized that we're safe."

Rémy nodded. "Delayed reaction, *chérie*. Totally normal."

She sighed. "I thought I was stronger than this."

Rémy pulled her close to kiss the top of her head. "My fierce goddess. It's all right that you were afraid."

"You weren't," she muttered as he leaned over to check the locks.

Rémy paused and looked at her gravely. "Yes, I was, more afraid than I've ever been in my life. *Mon coeur*, I don't know what I would have done if he'd hurt you." Rémy's voice was hoarse. "Killed you." His expression was tortured, and he looked suddenly haggard, all of the cool confidence she'd seen before melting away to show his true feelings.

She touched his cheek. "I'm fine, Rémy, thanks to you," she reassured him.

He looked like he wanted to say more, but one of the officers tapped on the window and he turned away with a grimace. "I'll get this done as quickly as possible," he promised as he hopped out, then he shut the door on the chaos outside, leaving her alone in the warm quiet of the car.

She watched everything for a while, him speaking and gesturing while the police took notes. She took out her phone and quickly texted Marina to tell her friend she couldn't meet her for drinks and that she'd explain later. She was just dozing off when he returned, and she saw that the police were getting back into their cars. She looked up in surprise. "I thought they wanted to talk to me, too?"

Rémy's expression was satisfied. "They agreed to take your statement at the station tomorrow."

"Isn't that unusual?" she asked as he helped her out of the car again.

He raised his eyebrows. "Didn't you hear? I'm a tycoon. We tycoons get what we want." He spoiled the effect by chuckling. "And I told them you weren't feeling well."

She smiled gratefully. "I *am* feeling sort of drained," she admitted.

"That's also a normal reaction. You were at least slightly in shock, and now your body is recovering," Rémy answered.

She turned toward him again. "How do you know this?" She paused, thinking, then continued. "And how the heck did you know just what to do when that boy — you know, came after us?"

He shrugged, that non-committal Gallic shrug that she was coming to both love and hate. "This… When you're in the position that my family is in, these things sometimes happen. I know I told you a little about the dangers, though not much. We were trained from a very young age, and we surround ourselves with highly-trained security, like Marc, who only acts as a driver for convenience. I have a black belt in karate, I've studied judo and Krav Maga, and I'm also a crack shot with pistols and rifles."

Annelise gaped at him.

He watched her face carefully, so she tried not to betray her horror, but she feared she hadn't been successful.

"Does it bother you so much?" he asked, the question hanging in the quiet of the car.

She shook her head, choosing her words carefully. "Not in the way you think. I hate that you have had to learn so much to defend yourself, just because of who you are. I don't hate that these are things you're obviously good at. I don't know what would have happened tonight if you hadn't been. That man came out of nowhere."

"I'm not a violent man," he said, and his face was impassive, but his eyes were still somehow vulnerable. Defensive.

"I know that," she said. "Of course I know that. You're exquisitely gentle, Rémy."

He nodded, satisfied. "Well, good. Now, do you want to head to your place or mine? I'm staying in Copley Square." He mentioned a neighborhood close to hers, near her work. "They said that we unfortunately can't visit Charles until the morning, for security reasons, but he's doing well. I'm guessing your haughty little feline friend is going to be wanting dinner by now."

She leaned against his shoulder, picturing Penelope's ornery face. "You're right. She'll be furious. She gets wet food in the evenings."

Annelise had almost forgotten Marc had slid into the car at the same time Rémy had until he leaned forward to tell the other man they were going to Annelise's. She leaned forward too, and to the side so she could see him.

"Marc, I don't know how to thank you. You have my utmost gratitude, from the bottom of my heart." His face looked as impassive as ever, but she could tell from his gruff voice when he answered that he wasn't displeased.

"Part of the job," he answered.

Impulsively, she squeezed his shoulder, and they exchanged a look in the rearview mirror. It was more than a job. She knew it, but she'd let it be.

They were back at her place almost as soon as they'd left the other house, and Rémy helped her out of the car, a gesture for which she was grateful as she still felt a little unsteady.

Annelise and Rémy held hands as they walked back up to her apartment. For her part, Annelise didn't want to be away from Rémy, didn't want to stop touching him, reassuring herself that they were safe.

He pulled his phone from his pocket and glanced at the multitude of messages that looked like they were streaming in.

"I called my brothers and Villiers," he explained. "Marc is heading back to the police station to meet one of Villiers' contacts. The young man is awake and in good condition, just bruised. They think they have a lead on where Claude has been masterminding some of his more illicit activities and that they can convince the kid to talk."

"That's good news, right?" she asked, puzzled by how worried he still looked.

"It's good news," he confirmed. "I just... I'll believe it when it really happens, you know? This seems...too easy."

Annelise raised both eyebrows. "Charles being held hostage and us almost getting shot was too easy?" she asked.

His laughter was dry. "I guess when you put it that way...perhaps I *am* being overly paranoid."

She leaned into him, wrapping her arms around his lean waist. "Perhaps," she agreed, "but I like you that way."

"You do?" he asked, surprised.

She nodded. "Definitely. You get this serious little wrinkle between your eyes, and your mouth looks stern. It's pretty sexy, actually. Kinda John Wayne meets Viggo Mortensen."

Rémy's laughter rolled through the entire stairwell, echoing off the marble walls. "Ah, *bébé*, you always know just the right thing to say."

As they walked to her doorway, he paused again, and Annelise turned questioningly. "For the record, you do like John Wayne and Viggo Mortensen, right?"

Annelise smiled at him from under her eyelashes. "Love them," she answered, continuing to walk and swinging her hips, knowing he was watching, before she unlocked and opened her front door.

Just as she'd hoped, he caught up to her almost instantly, spinning her around and kissing her lightly, pushing the door closed behind them with his foot.

"Do you have a cowboy hat in the closet?" he asked, waggling his eyebrows suggestively.

She couldn't prevent her peal of laughter at his hopeful expression. "Definitely later," she said. And the mental image of Rémy wearing a cowboy hat and nothing else was darn appealing. "But for now, I just want you." She paused, thinking about how scared she'd been. Terrified. "I *need* you."

Rémy opened his arms and she stepped into them, feeling like she was exactly where she was meant to be. "Always, *chérie*. Anything for you. Anything."

Chapter Fifteen

Holding Annelise again, thinking about how close he'd come to losing her — to losing his own life — Rémy was filled with gratitude at their good fortune and determined not to be too scared ever again to take a chance with his feelings. Life was just too short, and too precious, not to be lived.

When she moved against him slightly, though, every other thought fled from his mind but how good she felt. Warm, curvy, soft and smelling like heaven. Annelise.

He tipped her head back with one finger and kissed her like he was sipping at the finest, rarest Burgundy. Her taste was sweet and spicy, just like the woman herself, an intriguing mix of contradictions. As they kissed, he shrugged off his own coat and gently removed hers, letting them fall to the floor. When he pulled her against him again, this time separated only by the thin layers of their clothes, he could feel her nipples tighten to hard points against his chest, and it made his already hard cock grow impossibly thicker with arousal. He'd never been as turned on before in his life, not even when he was a teenager and it seemed like all he had to do was sneeze to get hard. But with Annelise, everything she did made him crazy. She was like his own personal fantasy.

She looked up at him, a mysterious, sexy smile playing on her lips. Yeah, she definitely felt him poking into her stomach. Instead of leaning in, though, she stepped back and settled down onto her knees. He could hardly believe it, but his fantasy goddess had just gotten even hotter.

"I want to taste you again," she whispered. "Do you mind?" The sight of her, kneeling in front of him on the floor of her living room, was almost too much for him. He barely stopped himself from shooting off, right there in his pants.

"I told you… You can do anything you want to any part of my body," he managed to croak. Her eyes went hot and she licked her plump, pink lips as she unzipped his pants, like she was looking forward to eating a lollipop. *Dieu*, but she was sexy as all hell.

His cock sprang free of his pants and underwear, popping up and straining toward her as she released him. He groaned when he felt the warmth of her breath, and nearly lost his balance when she suddenly took all his length into the molten wet velvet of her mouth. He started panting when she circled the base of his cock with her hand. It felt amazing. *She* felt amazing.

She stopped and looked up at him, making every nerve in his body scream. "Are you okay?" she asked, that cute little wrinkle appearing between her eyes.

"So damn good… Never want you to stop," he grunted.

Her concern changed to satisfaction. His woman knew how much she was pleasing him.

She sucked him into her mouth again then released him with a loud pop, making him groan again.

"You like that?" she asked, and he wasn't sure he liked the mischievous glint in her eyes.

"God, yes," he answered, stroking her silky hair.

She engulfed him again, this time swirling her magical tongue all around his girth, and he tensed, about to come right there in her mouth, but she released him again.

"Unhh," he moaned, torn between total arousal and absolute frustration.

"Mmm...I like this game," she said, and this time, he definitely thought the look in her eyes boded ill for him.

"You do, huh?" In one smooth motion, he picked her up and threw her onto the couch behind her. He pulled off her shoes, socks, pants and panties all at once. He wasn't sure where they landed or whether he'd torn them, and, frankly, he didn't care. All he cared about was baring her pretty pussy.

When he gently pushed her legs open, he found her pink folds glistening with moisture. *Arousal.*

"So beautiful," he breathed, before he bent his head to her.

She gasped his name as he began to lick her, drinking and lapping at her sex until she was panting with pleasure. He listened to her every sound, gauging what she liked the best and giving her more until she tightened her thighs and tensed, screaming her pleasure. He continued licking her lazily until she stopped trembling, savoring every drop of her spicy, salty taste.

When she seemed to catch her breath, she let her thighs fall open and glared at him. "No fair!" she complained, but her flushed cheeks and sparkling eyes told him she wasn't really mad.

"Compromise?" he offered.

She pursed her lips, pretending to consider. "I'm listening."

Rémy stood up and took off his shirt and undershirt, knowing that his hard cock was bobbing in front of her face as he moved. Her avid gaze darted from his cock to his chest, and he felt a glow of satisfaction. "I'll make it up to you if you take off your shirt and get up on your knees so I can fuck you so hard that you'll forget everything else."

Annelise sucked in a breath and her eyes went dark with arousal.

He smiled. "I love seeing what my dirty talk does to you. You want more?"

Her chest rose and fell rapidly, and her cheeks flushed a dark rose. She gave a jerky nod.

"Then show me those pretty nipples...now," he ordered.

She sat up and pulled off her sweater then unfastened her bra, letting her breasts bobble free. He reached out both hands to tweak the already-distended peaks.

"So sexy. They're hard just for me, aren't they?" he mused, and she nodded again, seeming mesmerized by what he was doing.

"Now, get up on your knees and show me that sexy ass," he ordered again. Annelise did what he asked, but she gave a sassy wiggle, making the globes of her ass jiggle enticingly.

"Aw, *bébé*. No fair. You know what watching your fine ass move does to me," he groaned, palming his cock.

"I want you inside me, Rémy," she said, looking back over her shoulder at him with eyes that were almost pleading. "So deep."

It was that last phrase that pushed him over the edge. With a hoarse cry, he plunged into her slick channel, feeling her tighten around him.

"Perfect, *mon coeur*. Like you were made for me," he groaned, starting a slow rhythm, punctuating each stroke with a light slap on the wobbling cheeks of her ass.

The sounds she made were driving him crazy, little gasps and squeaks of surprised pleasure, until he had to speed up. He reached around her, squeezing and massaging her breasts and nipples, and she cried out.

"Yes, yes, Rémy, oh my God!"

Spurred by her noises, he went faster and faster, hearing the couch thump on the ground but not caring. Nothing else mattered but Annelise. Her liquid heat was like nothing he'd ever felt, and as he moved in her, joining them, he didn't think he'd ever known such a sense of rightness. Bringing his woman pleasure, feeling her, *loving* her, was all that mattered. Nothing else existed but Annelise, connected to him so intimately. His cock swelled so he dragged all along every inch of her passage, and she let out breathy little moans that drove him even crazier.

Just when he thought he might go off without her, she screamed and tensed, her inner muscles clamping down around him. With that, he let himself go as well, shooting his seed deep into her with thrust after thrust, shaking and shuddering with the force of his pleasure.

Her core rippled around his cock, milking every last creamy drop from him, until they both collapsed onto the couch. He managed to turn them so that he curled behind his woman instead of landing on top of her, his cock still buried deep inside.

* * * *

Annelise woke slowly, confused but not unpleasantly. Rémy was behind her, like a hot, naked furnace. And there was a rich velvet fabric right in front of her face, like the fabric of her couch. Looking around, she saw the tall windows, the little details on the ceiling, and remembered where she was…in her living room, squished in front of Rémy on her own couch, nude. With a smile of feminine satisfaction, she remembered how they'd gotten there and why she had soreness in even more places she'd just learned existed on her body. *Holy cow*, Rémy had been frenzied last night, like a wild man. *Her* wild man.

She was grateful one of them had managed to at least pull a throw blanket over them, or they would have been chilly. She vaguely remembered Rémy getting up to feed an indignant Penelope, earning himself a furry friend for life, before coming back with a blanket. She supposed it made sense that they'd fallen asleep — deep satisfaction mixed with exhaustion could do that. She could still hear Rémy's faint snore, and his heavy breathing ruffled her hair. When she tried to gently wiggle free without waking him, the snoring stopped.

She moved again, and this time she felt something hard, growing harder and longer, against her butt.

"There is nothing better than waking pressed against you, Annelise," Rémy breathed, nuzzling her neck and giving her goosebumps.

She smiled and turned, and he kissed her cheek too but couldn't quite reach her lips. "Good morning. I can feel that one part of you, in particular, really likes being pressed up against me."

Rémy's chuckle rumbled in his chest against her back. "Well, yes, but that part of me always likes you — touching you, looking at you, thinking about you. He's easy. Kind of an Annelise compass, really. Always pointing at you."

Annelise laughed at how silly he was being and tried to turn more onto her back, but instead nearly pushed Rémy off the couch. He grabbed at her, ending up sort of hugging her while they both laughed.

"Ah, *chérie*. I want every morning to be like this," Rémy said as he settled behind her again, wrapping himself around her so she felt safe, warm and cherished.

Annelise tensed, unsure how to respond. She wanted it, too, but there was still so much to talk about.

"What is it?" Rémy asked, obviously feeling her tension.

And that was the question. Was her love going to be enough? Was she brave enough to ask about living together, and brave enough to hear the answer, whatever it was? All Annelise had to do was remember the sight of the young man, coming toward them, and she knew she could. She needed to.

"I want that, too, Rémy. But…how are we going to do it?"

"It's easy," he said, and she could hear he was smiling although she couldn't see his face. "We just pick a place and live there."

She wiggled again, and this time Rémy stood up so she could sit, too, before he settled himself next to her with his arm around her.

She looked at him. "I'm serious. You have a job and a life in Montreal, and I have a job and a life here in Boston. You have obligations and family and friends, and I do too. We're from different worlds, and different countries, too."

Rémy still smiled at her, and she thought his smile might have widened. She began to feel like she was missing something. "What is it? Why aren't you even a little concerned?"

"I'm not concerned because, well, didn't you wonder about the rest of what I was going to say yesterday? Why I found you here in Boston?"

How in the world did he manage to look so good first thing in the morning? Even with his hair mussed, and with his lap covered by a purple blanket, Rémy was the sexiest thing Annelise had ever seen. Then his words registered.

"I guess I just thought you wanted to find me to apologize, to see how I felt, if I could forgive you. And, um, I guess you got your answer."

Rémy smiled and took her hand into his larger one, bringing it briefly to his lips. "Yes, and you had your answer, too. But there was more. I had already been considering it, but when my last thoughts were of you when I thought I might not survive the attack—in spite of how we parted—I decided to go for it. I was offered a research position at one of the best universities in Boston, and I took it."

"What?" Annelise said, her mouth hanging open. She wanted to be totally sure she'd heard correctly because it was almost too good to be true.

The grin he gave her matched her own exuberant mood. "I'm moving to Boston — at least for a while, long enough for us to decide where we both want to be permanently. Together. I was already looking at places, and I got one of those long-term apartment hotel rooms. That's why Marc came along, too, and brought one of our armored cars. This isn't meant to be a short trip. Didn't you think it was a little extravagant, even for me?"

Her laugh was loud in the quiet room. "Well, yes, but you're a, like, kazillionaire, so what do I know about how you people live?"

Rémy's answering chuckle was deeply amused. "*Bébé*, I may be a kazillionaire, but it's having you that makes me feel truly rich. I love you."

The room went suddenly blurry as Annelise's eyes filled with tears. "Oh, Rémy! I love you too!" she said, throwing her arms around him. He wrapped his arms around her and pulled her onto his lap.

"Oh my God, we can really do this! I can't believe you were willing to move to Boston, not even knowing my answer." All she saw in his eyes was love and tenderness. No hesitation.

"I hoped, *chérie*, and I prayed. And now, realizing how close I came to losing you yesterday, I think I already knew that I loved you, maybe since the first moment I saw you. I would go much farther for you, you have to know that. We can go wherever we want."

"Wait, but you really enjoy what you'd be doing, too, right? I hope this isn't just...for me."

Rémy's smile was lopsided. "I will admit that Boston has some of my favorite historical research subjects and sources, along with my favorite modern subject…you. So yes, it's about you, and us, but also something I'm doing for myself."

A crazy, incandescent happiness grew inside her, until she thought she might be glowing. Rémy had already been planning to move to Boston! There wasn't anything preventing them from being together! He loved her. She loved him.

"Aaaahh!" she screamed, and Rémy jumped a little, but then chuckled again at her expression.

"Happy, my Annelise? You're so hard to read," he teased.

"Yes, yes, yes!" she exclaimed, getting up on her knees next to him on the couch. Rémy grinned, his teeth flashing white, and she peppered his face with kisses, punctuating each word until he was laughing again.

"I love you, *mon coeur*. My heart, anywhere and always," he said, pulling her close.

"I love you, too, Rémy. Anywhere and always," she answered — and kissed him again.

Want to see more like this?
Here's a taster for you to enjoy!

Rules of Engagement: Always Faithful
Caitlyn Willows

Excerpt

Staff Sergeant Rowan McKinley studied the steel warehouse from every angle she could see. Since her only viewpoint was from Charlie's battered old truck, that wasn't easy. The security lights being out made it doubly hard. There wasn't another person around or any sign of another vehicle. No activity whatsoever. Everyone and everything was tucked away for the evening, as it should be at midnight.

She glanced at the man beside her. The darkness kept her from seeing his face clearly, but she knew it would be lit with excitement. For lack of a better term, she could almost smell the testosterone in the air. *Or is that beer?* She'd swear he'd been drinking, even if she didn't want to admit that to herself.

It was all Rowan could do to keep from shaking. What in the world had she been thinking to come here? She was a legal specialist, not an MP, not CID and certainly not NCIS. Her stubborn determination to prove herself right had gotten her into this mess—a dangerous mess at that. And if Charlie *had* been drinking, she had been even stupider to get into a vehicle with him.

Rowan wiped her sweaty palms on her camouflage trousers. Her heart pounded so hard she'd swear he could hear it.

Where were her priorities? She had a child to think about. Why should she care if someone was stealing government property? She'd reported her suspicions to anyone and everyone who would listen. Why in the world couldn't she have left it at that? She'd done her duty.

But no… Like a modern-day *Don Quixote*, she'd had to go tilting at windmills. All things considered, her sanity was as questionable as that foolish old coot's.

She studied the hulking white building once more. No guards walking their posts. It looked quiet enough—safe, despite the lack of security lights. It should have put her at ease, but it only set her nerves on edge.

"Charlie, I don't like this. It doesn't seem right. I think we should leave."

He chuckled and gave her a playful slug on the arm. "You're being silly." After drawing his pistol, he slid from the truck and silently made his way to the building. *Easy to be brave when you're a walking giant.*

Rowan frowned when he walked inside. The door wasn't even locked. Now that was odd. *Too easy. A trap?* Possibly. Charlie was too gung-ho or too inebriated to notice—or maybe he embraced the challenge, the danger, the rush.

Rowan glanced around. She was a sitting target.

She searched the floorboard debris of to-go cups for something to use as a weapon. Nothing, not even a floor mat. For one brief second, she considered cranking the engine and getting out of there but dismissed the cowardly plan. She would not leave Charlie. They were safer together.

Curling her fingers around the door handle, she shoved her shoulder against the truck door. It groaned as it opened, announcing her presence to anyone who might have doubted it before.

Crouching low, Rowan ran to the building and ducked inside. Darkness enveloped her. Pitch black. Smothering. Her heartbeat thudded in her ears. Panic clutched at her stomach. In vain, she fought the claustrophobia, the overwhelming fear, the need to battle her way free and the urge to scream out her frustration.

Arms wrapped around her midsection. She stood frozen and lost. She heard scuffling off to her right. There was a blur—a sense rather than sight of movement. Then pain shattered through her head.

Home of Erotic Romance

Sign up for our newsletter and find out about all our romance book releases, eBook sales and promotions, sneak peeks and FREE romance books!

About the Author

Aurora is originally from the frozen tundra of the upper-Midwest (ok, not frozen all the time!) but now loves living in New England with her real-life hero/husband, two wonderfully silly sons, and one of the most extraordinary cats she has ever had the pleasure to meet. But she still goes back to the Midwest to visit, just never in January.

She doesn't remember a time that she didn't love to read, and has been writing stories since she learned how to hold a pencil. She has always liked the romantic scenes best in every book, story, and movie, so one day she decided to try her hand at writing her own romantic fiction, which changed her life in all the best ways.

Aurora loves to hear from readers. You can find her contact information, website details and author profile page at https://www.totallybound.com